Closing her eyes into the sun produced dancing flashes of orange, red, and yellow bursts behind her lids. An insect chirped and the repetitive sound lulled her hypnotically. Soon she lapsed into a half sleep, and a scene took form behind her closed lids.

Hundreds of armed men and horses battled on a field. Swords clashed and arrows flew. She was peering out of eyes that were not her own. A veil of blood splashed before her as a soldier crumpled to the ground. An anguished cry of pain grabbed her attention and spun her around. "Nooo!" someone shouted, and she had the feeling she was the one who had spoken.

Then she felt herself seem to lift into the air. Glancing down, she saw the whole panorama of the violent battle, and directly below her, she saw a soldier fall. His armor was sprayed with blood. As his knees buckled beneath him, he threw back the metal visor of his helmet and gazed upward, torment written across his features.

Her eyes snapped open. Once again she was in the tranquil forest, but her heart was pounding. She searched in every direction, looking for signs of battle. Only the gentle noises of nature surrounded her.

Once upon a Time

THE NIGHT DANCE

A Retelling of "The Twelve Dancing Princesses"

BY SUZANNE WEYN

SIMON PULSE
New York   London   Toronto   Sydney

This book is a work of fiction. Any references to historical events, real people,
or real locales are used fictitiously. Other names, characters, places, and incidents
are the product of the author's imagination, and any resemblance to actual
events or locales or persons, living or dead, is entirely coincidental.

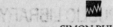

SIMON PULSE

An imprint of Simon & Schuster Children's Publishing Division
1230 Avenue of the Americas, New York, NY 10020
Copyright © 2005 by Suzanne Weyn
All rights reserved, including the right of
reproduction in whole or in part in any form.
SIMON PULSE and colophon are registered trademarks
of Simon & Schuster, Inc.
The text of this book was set in Adobe Jenson.
Manufactured in the United States of America
This Simon Pulse edition November 2008
2 4 6 8 10 9 7 5 3 1
Library of Congress Control Number 2005921498
ISBN-13: 978-1-4169-6132-1
ISBN-10: 1-4169-6132-1

*For Bethany Buck,
with deep appreciation for all your support,
encouragement, and laughter through the years,
not to mention the great lunches*

TABLE OF CONTENTS

PROLOGUE
1

PART ONE: *Mystic Realms*

CHAPTER ONE: *Once upon a Time . . .*
7

CHAPTER TWO: *The Lost Lady of the Lake*
16

CHAPTER THREE: *Rowena's Escape*
24

CHAPTER FOUR: *Sir Bedivere, the Last Knight of the Round Table*
28

CHAPTER FIVE: *Eleanore the Observant*
35

CHAPTER SIX: *Rowena's Scrying Bowl*
39

CHAPTER SEVEN: *Morgan le Fey Watches*
45

PART TWO: *The Night Moves*

CHAPTER EIGHT: *Vivienne's Call*
51

CHAPTER NINE: *Rowena's Search*
53

CHAPTER TEN: *Sir Bedivere No More*
57

CHAPTER ELEVEN: *Eleanore's Earring*
62

CHAPTER TWELVE: *Sir Ethan's Outrage*
67

CHAPTER THIRTEEN: *Rowena Meets Millicent*
70

CHAPTER FOURTEEN: *Bedivere's Fight*
75

CHAPTER FIFTEEN: *Rowena*
82

CHAPTER SIXTEEN: *Morgan Follows*
93

PART THREE: *The Enchanted Ones*

CHAPTER SEVENTEEN: *Vivienne's Despair*
105

CHAPTER EIGHTEEN: *Bedivere in Love*
107

CHAPTER NINETEEN: *Sir Ethan's Next Plan*
110

CHAPTER TWENTY: *Eleanore Revolts*
116

CHAPTER TWENTY-ONE: *Bedivere Is Tempted*
123

PART FOUR: *The Contest*

CHAPTER TWENTY-TWO: *Eleanore Wields Her Potion*
133

CHAPTER TWENTY-THREE: *Rowena Objects*
142

CHAPTER TWENTY-FOUR: *Bedivere Takes His Turn*
150

CHAPTER TWENTY-FIVE: *Morgan Gets Serious*
154

CHAPTER TWENTY-SIX: *Bedivere Finds His Way*
157

CHAPTER TWENTY-SEVEN: *Morgan the Bat*
163

CHAPTER TWENTY-EIGHT: *Vivienne's Chance*
165

CHAPTER TWENTY-NINE: *Bedivere Disappears*
167

CHAPTER THIRTY: *Princess Rowena*

170

CHAPTER THIRTY-ONE: *Bedivere Is Trapped*
174

CHAPTER THIRTY-TWO: *Three Forests*
177

CHAPTER THIRTY-THREE: *Encounters*
183

EPILOGUE
189

Then loudly cried the bold Sir Bedivere,
"Ah! my Lord Arthur, whither shall I go?
Where shall I hide my forehead and my eyes?
For now I see the true old times are dead,
When every morning brought a noble chance,
And every chance brought out a noble knight.
Such times have been not since the light that led
The holy Elders with the gift of myrrh.
But now the whole ROUND TABLE is dissolved
Which was an image of the mighty world;
And I, the last, go forth companionless,
And the days darken round me and the years,
Among new men, strange faces, other minds."

From *Morte d' Arthur* by Alfred Lord Tennyson

PROLOGUE

Rowena pressed her slim body into the cool shadowy corner of the high wall in the empty courtyard. Shaded by the towering building behind her, her wavy copper-colored hair seemed to take on a more auburn hue. A determined glint deepened her lively, celery-colored eyes into a stormy blue-green.

Furtively glancing back at the towering manor that was her home, she saw one of her eleven sisters, Eleanore, peer out from a high, narrow window. Even from this distance she could read the look of longing in her sister's expression. Prickly though Eleanore could be, Rowena still sympathized with the trapped restlessness she knew her sister felt. Still, she couldn't take the chance of being seen, and she shrank back farther into the shadows.

Rawkeeeee! Rowena's hand suddenly flew to her heart as she whirled toward an open kitchen window on the first floor of the manor. The panicked squawk of a captive pheasant had made her jump.

Helen, the cook, appeared in the window with a small axe held high over her head and the bird clasped firmly in her other hand. She ended the struggling creature's life swiftly with a strong, well-placed blow to its neck against a chopping board. Then she strode away from the table by the window with the beheaded pheasant in her arms, setting about the business of preparing the bird for roasting.

When Rowena turned her attention back to the upper window, Eleanore was no longer there. In the next minute, Helen reappeared at the kitchen window, but only for a second, to pull the shutters closed.

Rowena waited, barely breathing, for several minutes more. Soon she felt confident that things were finally as she had hoped they'd be at this hour. Her sisters would be busy with their weaving and embroidery. Their father, Sir Ethan of Colchester, was reviewing his monthly accounts, a process that usually took hours. Most likely he wouldn't lift his head from his books until Mary, the head housemaid, summoned him for dinner.

Reaching into the cobalt blue velvet cape she wore against the late spring's still-cool breezes, Rowena withdrew a small iron cleaver that she'd smuggled from the kitchen. Even in this shadowed spot, its blade gleamed. Her father's military past had left him with a love of rules, order, and efficiency. Among his many dictates to the servants was his insistence that they regularly sharpen all the household blades on a whetstone.

A scuffle at her feet caused her eyes to dart downward. She immediately jumped back, startled by a tiny gray field mouse that had scurried in through the narrow opening that rose from the base of the wall in an inverted v-shape. The creature paused for a moment to stare up at her, then zigzagged its way across the courtyard, probably headed for the kitchen.

When her heart had settled, Rowena turned again toward the wall. With eager fingers, she traced the lines of a crack that traveled from the top of the break in the wall halfway up to the top. Several fissures snaked out from the main fracture, further weakening this section of the enclosure.

The day before, when Mary had ordered two of the house boys to remove a brown, dead, potted tree—one of the many potted plants adorning the slate-tiled courtyard—from this corner of the courtyard, Rowena had first noticed the break in the wall. She instantly recognized the opportunity she'd been hoping for.

With the cleaver in her firm grip, she attempted several slow practice passes to be sure that when the moment was right, her aim would be accurate. Then, wrapping her fingers around the cleaver's iron handle, she waited, her back pressed against the wall.

In the next moment, the bell from the monastery outside the nearby town of Glastonbury chimed as it always did at this hour, calling the monks to prayer.

Now! Rowena thought wildly. She smashed the

cleaver's blade down into the line of the crack, the deeply satisfying crash masked by the resonating bell.

The cleaver stuck fast into the wall. With two hands, she frantically yanked it out and struck again.

And now!

And now!

Again and again, she savagely wielded the blade into the cracks, straining every lean muscle of her lithe body. With each blow her joy mounted as the crumbling powdery stone tumbled to her feet.

The bell ceased its summoning toll.

Dropping to her knees, Rowena took a quick moment to recover from her violent effort and then pushed the debris away from the opening. She lay flat on her stomach and rolled onto her right shoulder. From this vantage point it was immediately apparent that even if she managed to get her head through the opening, her shoulders would never make it.

Rowena rolled back up into a crouch and then slowly stood, resolving not to give in to disappointment. The monastery bell would chime again tomorrow, and the next day, and the day after that, just as it had rung at the same hour on every day of her life. There would be other chances to chip away at this wall, the cursed barrier that had closed her off from the wide, glorious world for the past twelve years, since the time when her mother had left them.

PART ONE

Mystic Realms

CHAPTER ONE
Once upon a Time . . .

. . . Ethan of Colchester found himself lost in a towering primeval forest. Although he had not wandered far from his military encampment, he was now strangely at a loss as to how to return to it.

While camped with his fellow soldiers, he'd spied a boar rustling through the underbrush. He immediately imagined the wild, tusked pig roasting over an open flame, a succulent meal for hungry men. Withdrawing his knife from his belt, he also grabbed his spear and set off after the creature.

He'd learned his expert hunting skills from his grandfather, who had been a Roman legionnaire during the last days that Imperial Rome ruled over Britain. Slaying this boar promised to be an easy task.

Yet every time Ethan came within striking range, the boar mysteriously reappeared several yards farther on. Frustrated, but determined, he continued to pursue the animal, convinced that the wavering, dappled light filtering through the ancient trees was simply playing tricks on his eyes. He chased the boar over a hill and down an embankment that led to a place less densely crowded with trees.

The boar stood in a patch of sunlight as if awaiting him.

Ethan halted, perplexed. What was happening? Why had the elusive animal suddenly grown so still?

Before Ethan's astonished eyes, the boar began to roll on its back and belly, its tusks flashing as it grunted frantically, and while it performed this frenetic act, a glistening pond began to spread underneath its portly, graceless body.

Spear raised, Ethan cautiously approached the scuffling boar. With each step, the ground beneath his boots grew increasingly muddy. In a moment, he stood in an ever-deepening puddle of water. He gazed around, dumbstruck with wonder, as the puddle became a knee-deep pond and then rapidly continued to increase for a great distance.

Slabs of land were thrust up at odd angles under the force of the expanding water. A tremendous flat boulder heaved up from beneath the cracked earth, jutting into the new lake and forming a natural dock.

So great was Ethan's amazement that he momentarily forgot about the boar. When he finally checked for it, he saw that, in the place where it had been, a woman now stood in water that rose to just below her bosom.

White blond hair waved down to her slender shoulders and fanned out around her on the water. Vivid blue eyes shone from her beautiful pale face.

An almost sheer, powder blue shift, banded under her breasts with golden cord, clung to her. Her form beneath the clinging fabric was increasingly visible as she moved toward him through the shimmering lake.

When they were face to face, with the water swirling around them, the woman ran her hand along the sleeve of his rough tunic and rested her head on his shoulder, her hair cascading down. "I knew you would come," she said softly.

Ethan put his hard soldier's hand on the back of her neck and stroked her impossibly soft hair, his once untamed heart now completely captive.

Ethan was never certain if his great love for Vivienne was real or a magical enchantment. He didn't much care, either.

With his own hands, he built a home of stone and wood there in the ancient forest beside the lake that had appeared on the day he'd first encountered Vivienne. When a traveling monk came to them one day, desperate for directions back to the road, Ethan prevailed upon him to perform a wedding, uniting the two lovers as husband and wife. As soon as the marriage ceremony was completed, the monk stumbled away from them, suddenly seeming to know how to leave the forest.

Within nine months, Vivienne gave birth to twin daughters whom they named Mathilde and Eleanore. The next nine months brought another set of twin girls, Chloe and Bronwyn. In three years more,

Vivienne gave birth to Ione and Isolde, Cecily and Helewise, Gwendolyn and Brianna, Ashlynn and Rowena; twelve daughters in all, six sets of twins. In little less than five years, Ethan became the father of twelve children all under the age of five.

Vivienne ran her lively, sometimes chaotic, brood with astounding ease. A toddler leaning too far out a window was mysteriously drawn back inside with a firm look from Vivienne. Any cranky cry was instantly soothed by the melodies she crooned to them in her lilting, crystal voice.

For his part, Ethan worked ceaselessly, hunting, farming a small plot in the front yard, and fishing in the magical lake beside the house. He loved this life and his only source of concern was that Vivienne sometimes left for periods of time, usually in the evening once the girls were all asleep. She would step out the back door and walk off into the forest. When he questioned her upon her return several hours later, she always answered him in the same way: "Sometimes there are things I must do. Have no worry, dearest love. My heart is always with you and my twelve princesses."

Ethan loved and trusted his wife, so he didn't question her further. For ten years she left from time to time, but always came back. As long as Vivienne returned to him, Ethan was satisfied.

Except that one day she did not return.

Leaving the younger girls in the care of the older ones, Ethan went out to search for Vivienne. Two days later, hoarse from calling her name, he stumbled out of the forest and trudged down a dirt road. He walked until he collapsed from lack of food, water, and sleep.

When he awoke in a monastery another two days later, the monk, Brother Joseph, who had found him, claimed he'd been talking while he slept. "You were calling for a woman."

Ethan asked the monks if they knew anything of his wife, Vivienne. "It's a name we have heard tell of in druid myths and local legends," Brother Joseph said. "We believe you have been bewitched by a forest spirit."

"But I have children," Ethan objected, pulling himself upright on the plain cot on which he was lying.

"Most likely, you dreamed them," said Brother Joseph. "Forget about them. Stay here with us and count yourself blessed to be back in the world of reality."

Ethan was instantly on his feet, heading for the door. Before he was over the threshold, though, he collapsed once again.

The monk tended to him and in a day more, Ethan was once again strong. Although the monks of the monastery implored him to stay, insisting that his daughters were not real, Ethan was determined to get back to them.

Heading down the road, he recognized the spot where he had been encamped as a soldier ten years earlier. He entered the forest there and easily found his way toward his house. It seemed strange to him that he could have ever lost his way; it was so clear to him now. Indeed, it did seem as though some sort of fog had been lifted from his mind.

When he came over the embankment near where he lived, he stopped, a terrible fear gripping him. His house was below, where he had built it. But the glistening lake beside it was gone. Only the jutting boulder remained.

An overpowering terror seized him as he recalled what the monks had said. Perhaps these past ten years with Vivienne and his twelve beautiful daughters had never happened.

What if, all these years, he had been no more than a madman under a spell?

Maybe there never had been a lake in this spot.

Maybe there had been no Vivienne. No children.

With a pounding, frantic heart he raced down the hill, scattering leaves and branches in his desperate need to know the truth, no matter how terrible.

Throwing open the front door, he was greeted by the questioning gaze of twelve sets of hopeful young eyes seated at various places around the room. "Did you find mother?" Eleanore asked.

Words choked in his throat. He was so overcome with relief to see that his children were indeed real— to observe some small resemblance to their mother in each expectant, upturned face—that he collapsed into a chair and became engulfed with great, heaving sobs.

In that moment he somehow knew that these twelve daughters were all he had left of Vivienne.

Despair mingled with relief as he dropped his head into his hands and continued to sob disconsolately.

One by one the girls came to him, stroking and hugging him with their small, tender, consoling hands. This great figure of a heaving, sobbing man, their father, was all they had left as well.

Four months passed and Ethan finally stopped looking out the door at twilight, hoping for Vivienne's miraculous, improbable return. With his once fervent hopes at last fully faded, he decided to pack away her clothing and other things.

It was while cleaning out Vivienne's possessions that he came upon a carved wooden box hidden at the bottom of a trunk. Opening it, he discovered brilliant blue sapphires and gleaming diamonds inside. Pouring these gems into a leather hunting pouch, he traveled by foot to the nearby town of Glastonbury to see what this unexpected treasure would buy him. The girls followed him as far as the front doorway. "Stay put. I will return," he told them as he bolted the door.

Within two days he returned on horseback, leading a veritable army of artisans and ox-drawn carts carrying every sort of building supply. In the lead of this strange procession were axe-wielding men who hacked a wide swathe through the forest.

The twelve girls watched, both excited and a bit worried, while day after day the ground shook as additional trees were felled and the land cleared. The air rang with the hammering and banging of working men. Each day their lovely cottage expanded and grew, climbing higher here, widening there. Soon the original cottage lay in the center of a grand manor house. Masons surrounded this new home with a wall nearly ten feet high.

When the building was done, Ethan still had sapphires and diamonds remaining in his pouch. He used them to obtain marble flooring from Rome, mirrors framed in gold from the mines in Carmarthenshire, carved furniture from Norsemen of the Scandinavian Peninsula, and pottery and dishware imported from Asia and brought to Britain by the Romans. He bought bolts of fabrics from merchants who obtained them from the Normans and Franks across the Great English Channel. He procured linens, weavings, and dyed woolens from the Celts who traversed the Irish Sea. His girls would want for nothing.

Except freedom.

When the building and furnishing was finished, Sir Ethan shut the ornate, ten-foot wrought iron gate that connected both sides of the wall, bolting the lock with a resounding clang. Nothing would get in—and no one would get out.

Only Ethan would come and go from this lavish prison in the forest. Furnishing his new home had made him familiar with the ways of importing. Being so close to the Bristol Channel gave him easy access to the ships that arrived with goods from other places. With his remaining gems to start him off, Ethan was soon a thriving merchant of imports.

His twelve daughters, once so used to running barefoot through streams and building mud maidens beside their now-vanished lake, were shut in. Having lost Vivienne to the forest, Sir Ethan was determined to suffer no more losses.

CHAPTER TWO
The Lost Lady of the Lake

Vivienne gazed up from her watery prison below the lake's surface. Never had her determination to break free of the enchantment that trapped her there been greater.

In a dream, she had seen that her nephew, Arthur, leader of the united Seven Kingdoms of Britain, High King of Camelot, was in mortal danger.

She was the leader of the magical realm of Avalon, and Vivienne's visions were not the mere dreams of a sleeper. Through years of mystical study, she had cultivated her dreaming ability until it functioned as yet another way of seeing. Even now, locked away in an underground lake, important *dreams* still came to her.

And this *dream* disturbed her mightily. In it, Arthur was fighting for his life. Even the enchanted sword, Excalibur, that she had given him would not be powerful enough to protect him against his foe, Mordred.

Her kinswoman, Morgan le Fey, mistress of dark sorcery and Arthur's half sister, had sent her son, Mordred, into battle against Arthur. She had concocted a lethal poison into which Mordred had dipped the tip of his own sword.

Vivienne had sworn to her dying sister, Ingraine, Arthur's mother, that she would always protect young Arthur from harm. She had used her magic to fashion him a sword so magical that it would protect him from all bodily harm. It made Arthur invincible in battle and nearly immortal.

Creating Excalibur had been her crowning achievement. All her skill at harnessing the forces of nature and magic had gone into its formation. More than ever before, she was thankful for all she had learned from Merlin, the greatest wizard of the age.

Merlin had been a generous mentor, revealing to her secrets of magic and wizardry previously known only to him. But she paid a price for being his only student. There were those on Avalon who envied her friendship with the ancient sorcerer. As an excuse to attack her, they insisted that she be punished for intending to grant powers reserved for the mystic realm to a mortal.

In her own defense, Vivienne argued that Arthur was entitled to it as a son of Ingraine, a sorceress of Avalon. It didn't matter that his father was the chieftain Uther Pendragon, a mortal. Arthur's mother was from Avalon, and he was entitled to the protection of Avalon.

Vivienne's enemies were not swayed. Rumors spread that they plotted against her life.

She hid the sword away for the day when Arthur,

who was still a child, would require it. And then she made plans to hide in the mortal realm in order to escape the wrath of those she had angered.

Conjuring a spell, she wished for her perfect mortal lover. Ethan's face instantly appeared in the scrying bowl, the gold-lined vessel used in the old ways for magical seeing. The moment she laid eyes on his strong face she understood that, though he was only mortal, complete happiness would be hers if she could win him.

And win him, she did. At first, she used a spell to lure him and make him love her, but soon their union became the partnership of true soul mates.

Their life together exceeded her wildest hopes for happiness. She had children quickly, wanting to make up for the time she had lost as a childless woman of magic. She luxuriated in the oceanic pleasures of true love that she received from both her babes and her devoted husband. For ten years she lived an idyllic existence, hiding in the mortal world.

From time to time she would walk out of her cottage and use her scrying bowl to check on Arthur. The day finally came, however, when young Arthur's first sword, the one he pulled from the stone set in place by Merlin, was smashed in battle. Struggling valiantly, Arthur won the day even with half a sword, but he would require a new weapon.

He would need Excalibur.

So she set out to take Excalibur and its scabbard from its hiding place beneath the magical lake she had formed outside her cottage. She gave it to the young king as a gift, asking only that he return it to her upon his death.

For years Arthur prospered with Excalibur's help, uniting Britain, staving off outside invasions, building the glorious kingdom of Camelot, and creating the Round Table of revered and noble knights.

More years passed and she continued to observe Arthur's triumphs through her scrying bowl, keeping her word to her sister to make sure he stayed safe. But a time came when the vision she saw in her bowl was disturbing. Through magical trickery, Morgan le Fey had stolen Excalibur and given it to a knight named Accolon whom she had seduced. Vivienne saw that Morgan's plan was to have Accolon slay Arthur using Excalibur to do the job.

Rushing to Arthur's aid, Vivienne abruptly left the cottage one evening. Traveling by magic means, she found Morgan le Fey at Camelot with Accolon.

In a fury of spells and counterspells, curses and antidotes, they battled. Afraid, Accolon tried to rid himself of the sword and scabbard by throwing them into a nearby lake. Assuming a watery form, Vivienne disappeared below the surface to retrieve them. When she resurfaced her enemies had fled.

She was able to give the sword back to the grateful Arthur, but upon her return to her cottage home, she was ambushed by Morgan le Fey and Accolon. The knight plunged her into the lake while Morgan le Fey exercised her dark powers, sinking the lake many miles below the Earth's surface into a huge subterranean cavern and sealing it with an impenetrable surface, like a bubble of inescapable magic.

After falling, the lake seemed to settle. Vivienne could see that no sun filtered through the water. Only a pale glow from above reached her. It was even fainter than moonlight.

Vivienne quickly discovered that though she could hover near the top, she couldn't break through the surface of the water. It was as though it had been coated with some thickening agent that she could not penetrate.

What new magic was this? It confounded her. She sank again to the bottom, wondering what enchantment Morgan had conjured that could stump her in this way. For all her training, Vivienne had never seen a spell like this.

Did they think they had drowned her? Morgan had to know that water was Vivienne's element. She was as at home in it as a fish. In fact, that was why she had created the lake next to her cottage, because she could not stand to be too far from water.

Despite this, her kinswoman's magic proved surprisingly powerful and Vivienne's own powers had been weakened by her struggle with the sinister enchantress. No amount of focus or concentration was sufficient to free her from this watery prison.

The days passed as Vivienne tried to undo the spell that held her. Before long, she had exhausted all her counter charms and spells.

Not knowing what else to do, she languished there below the ground beside her cottage, so near and yet completely unable to contact those she loved so passionately.

If only she had her scrying bowl. But she had set it down at the foot of an ancient, gnarled tree before setting off on her quest to defeat Morgan le Fay and Accolon. With it she might at least observe how her little girls fared without her, how her beloved Ethan was managing in her absence.

She couldn't understand why one of her girls had not picked up the bowl by now. She hadn't left it far from the cottage. Certainly they were forever wandering through the woods. They had her restless, curious spirit and their father's fearless courage.

Something was keeping them away from it. She sensed it. And it made her afraid that some harm or imprisonment had befallen them. She hoped for a dream of them, but none came.

In time, a degree of strength returned to her. For a while, she spent all her energy directing magic at the seal that covered her. But Morgan's magic held fast there.

Finally giving up on that plan, she turned instead to the task of finding a side way out. Vivienne spent the next days of her imprisonment probing with her magic, and she had some success in blasting out watery tunnels.

She created a network of many paths under the ground. The tunnels would fill with water until they turned upward, above the water. From that point, the tunnels traveled through dry ground and under rock ledge, finally coming out to the natural cavern under the earth where her lake was now located.

With all her focus and memory of the landscape near her home, she continued to blast out tunnels. She clamped her eyes shut and tried to envision every tunnel, blasting out new ones that led out of the cavern.

She created these pathways with the diligence of a burrowing mole. She used her magic to fill each tunnel with the music of Avalon, music she remembered loving as a child. If she was ever able to escape, she wanted this magical music to be there to guide her way back to her cottage.

The last tunnel she dug with her magic would lead from the cavern right into a root cellar under her cottage—at least she hoped it did; she couldn't be sure. It was this last tunnel that inspired her to hope an escape might be possible.

When this last tunnel was completed, she headed toward the nearest underground opening, intending to travel up and into the cavern and to go from there to her cottage. But as soon as she got near the underwater entrance, she was thrown backward.

That impenetrable bubble that sealed her off from the surface was apparently all around her, not only above. Morgan had apparently learned her spell-making well. Even with the powerful training Vivienne had received in Avalon and from Merlin, she could not break through this enchantment.

She had to face the truth: She could not get out on her own. Someone from the outside would need to find a way to free her.

Closing her eyes, Vivienne touched the tips of her fingers together and focused her mind. Gone was the whirlwind of emotional torment, replaced by an imposed calm. Using the methods of mental discipline she had studied with Merlin, Vivienne concentrated on contacting her daughters.

At least one of them, if not all, must have inherited some of her mystical powers. She'd often noticed Rowena, the youngest of the girls—her baby—staring off into space with a faraway look in her beautiful green eyes as though she were seeing some vision from another time and place. It was a sure sign that she had the vision, and it was what Vivienne was now counting on.

CHAPTER THREE
Rowena's Escape

After weeks of chipping away at the opening, Rowena finally managed to squeeze her hips through the narrow break in the wall and draw her legs through to the other side. She stood and gazed at the giant pines surrounding her, feeling like a baby, newly born into a wonderful, wide world. She breathed deeply, drawing in the pungent fragrance of pine needles and bark, moss and mud.

She walked forward into the forest, calculating that she had about an hour before she would have to return. She'd told her sisters that Helen was teaching her to cook in the kitchen so she wouldn't be joining them for embroidery.

"Why do you want to cook?" her twin, Ashlynn, had questioned. "You won't ever need to cook."

Rowena had shrugged. "I'm bored of embroidery," she'd answered. That much, at least, had been true and from the slovenly work she produced, her sisters could well believe it.

"I think it would be fun to cook," her sister Brianna had said. "I'd love to have guests over and feed them and have big parties in the evenings. That's what I dream of. Oh, but Father never lets anyone near us. He's too frightened that a guest might sneak out with one of us hidden under his cloak."

Rowena took one more step and remembered that she wore the silk slippers her father had commissioned for them from a shoemaker in Glastonbury. Her father said the material was made by worms that spun it in far off Oriental lands. It had been brought by ship and cost him dearly.

The slippers were beautiful, made in shiny, deep, jewel tones, edged with delicate ribbon, and wonderfully comfortable; but they were not suited to outside wear since they tore easily and showed every bit of dirt. Since the sisters never went farther than the slate-tiled courtyard, they were fine. But a walk in the forest would destroy them and would reveal that she'd gone out. Removing the slippers, she stuck one in each pocket of her cloak and continued on, barefoot.

Without the benefit of shoes, Rowena had to pick her way carefully over rocks and fallen branches. She walked until she felt certain she could not be seen from any high manor window, then, shrugging off her cape and hanging it on a branch, she crawled up onto a large flat boulder that was drenched in sun and stretched out.

The rock was warm and felt good against her skin. She pushed up the long, draped, white sleeves of her gown to feel more of it against her.

Closing her eyes into the sun produced dancing

flashes of orange, red, and yellow bursts behind her lids. An insect chirped and the repetitive sound lulled her hypnotically. Soon she lapsed into a half sleep, and a scene took form behind her closed lids.

Hundreds of armed men and horses battled on a field. Swords clashed and arrows flew. She was peering out of eyes that were not her own. A veil of blood splashed before her as a soldier crumpled to the ground. An anguished cry of pain grabbed her attention and spun her around. "Nooo!" someone shouted, and she had the feeling she was the one who had spoken.

Then she felt herself seem to lift into the air. Glancing down, she saw the whole panorama of the violent battle, and directly below her, she saw a soldier. His armor was sprayed with blood. As his knees buckled beneath him, he threw back the metal visor of his helmet and gazed upward, torment written across his features.

Her eyes snapped open. Once again she was in the tranquil forest, but her heart was pounding. She searched in every direction, looking for signs of battle. Only the gentle noises of nature surrounded her.

Feeling unnerved by this violent vision, she slid off the rock, grabbed her cape, and hurried back to the wall. Once back in the courtyard, she pulled a potted tree in front of the opening to conceal it from view and put her slippers back on.

When she entered the sewing room where her sisters were, she sensed Eleanore scrutinizing her. Her eldest sister was keenly observant so Rowena was especially careful to appear normal and happy, joking with her sisters and betraying nothing. "How was the cooking class?" Ashlynn asked.

"Smelly," Rowena answered. "Don't come near me, I must reek of mutton stew."

At supper that night, the sisters joined their father, as they always did, at the long table in the high-ceilinged dining hall. The meal went on around her as she mechanically put food in her mouth, only half aware of the lively conversation her sisters were having regarding a new eight-foot-long tapestry, featuring a castle and a royal forest, that her father had had imported from France. "There's a prince depicted on it who is so manly," Mathilde gushed enthusiastically.

"He's fine, but I like the adorable unicorn that walks alongside the princess," Isolde offered. "Where will it hang, Father?"

"I was thinking of putting it right here in the dining hall," he replied.

Mathilde frowned. "I was hoping the prince could be in *our* room."

Sir Ethan raised an eyebrow and cast a wary glance at her. "I'd say it's definitely going into the dining hall."

Rowena liked the tapestry, but she was unable to care much about it. The soldier's face that she had seen in her vision haunted her. It was as if, in that moment, they had exchanged something mysterious and deep.

How could she feel so connected to a man she had never met?

CHAPTER FOUR
Sir Bedivere, the Last Knight of the Round Table

Bedivere bent low in order to hear Arthur more clearly. As he attuned his ear to the dying king's words, he gazed out over the corpse-strewn battlefield at Camlan. Fallen men from both sides of the horrific fight lay with their limbs still entangled in combat, their blood-soaked bodies turning the grass a blackish red. Their dead horses lay splayed and bleeding beside them.

He was not yet sure which side had won. It appeared that he and Arthur were the only two left alive. All the other knights of the Round Table now lay dead, their armor reflecting the pink light of the setting sun.

Mordred, who had raised this army against Arthur, was slain by Arthur's own hand. In that fight, Mordred had not fallen before dealing Arthur a severe wound, enhanced by a deadly poison at the point of his sword. It had been concocted for him, no doubt, by his witch mother, Morgan le Fey.

"One good thing can come of this for you," Arthur spoke in a fading, forced voice. Uncannily a glint of merriment had found its way into his dying eyes. "No longer will the minstrels call you the handsomest man on the island save King Arthur."

A blast of dark laughter escaped from Bedivere despite the dire circumstances. The minstrels who sang of the bold exploits of King Arthur and his noble knights of the Round Table always spoke of Bedivere as *most handsome save Arthur*. It had never bothered him; he was not naturally vain.

What *had* irked him was that, of late, they had begun referring to him as *Bedivere the one-handed*. He'd suffered a severed tendon during a particularly fierce battle and it had cost him the use of his left hand. He didn't want to be known as the *one-handed* because it implied weakness. The minstrels were quick to add, "Although he was one-handed, no three warriors drew blood in the same field faster than he." Nonetheless, Bedivere still found his ailment an embarrassment.

"So, most handsome one remaining on the island, I have something to ask of you," Arthur continued, the glint of mirth still alive on his strained, drawn face.

Bedivere shook his head. "I am not *yet* the most handsome," he replied. "And I would be glad never to have that title. Lean on me, and I can support you away from this bloody ground to where we can get you some care."

"There's no reason to move me," Arthur said, resisting Bedivere's attempt to raise him. "The wound I suffered to my head, the one dealt by Mordred, is too deep. Let what will be come to pass."

He lifted his sword, Excalibur, which he still

gripped at his side, several inches from the ground. "Take my sword and toss it into the middle of a lake. Return it to my kinswoman Vivienne, the Lady of the Lake. She who first gave it to me bade me promise I would never let it fall into any other hands but my own."

Bedivere turned in every direction. "Do you mean the river?" Bedivere asked, nodding toward the Camel River that ran under a nearby bridge.

Arthur shook his head and winced at the pain it caused him. "It must go back to the Lady of the Lake," he insisted.

Bedivere heard the crash of the ocean's surf against the rocky shore a short way off. "I'll plunge it in the sea, then," he suggested.

Arthur gripped Bedivere's arm with surprising strength and pulled himself up. "It must go back to the enchanted lake," he said, his eyes now burning with determination. "My soul cannot rest until this is done. Swear to me that you will return it to her. Swear!"

"I swear it," Bedivere promised as Arthur slumped back onto the ground, dead.

Bedivere sat down heavily on the chill ground beside Arthur, his friend and king. Excalibur gleamed in the sunlight, and the idea of using it to take his own life occurred to Bedivere. He should be dead; all his companions lay lifeless around him. It was merely some quirk of fate that he still lived.

He sat, feeling that the life was gone from him, that he was some freakish breathing corpse whose soul had gone off to accompany the departed soul of his king.

Reaching across Arthur's lifeless body, he lifted Excalibur from Arthur's loosened grip and laid it on his own knees. Its golden, bejeweled hilt glistened with diamonds and topaz.

How could he ever throw his king's weapon away into a lake? It should be hung on a wall as a remembrance of the greatest king the island of England had ever seen. But what wall? Arthur's castle at Camelot probably had already fallen to invading armies. There was no place for him to return to, no wall of honor on which to mount Arthur's sword. And besides—he had sworn to throw it in a lake.

"But what lake, Arthur?" he asked the dead companion beside him, addressing him as the friend he had been before becoming his king. "What lake?"

He sat beside Arthur for more than an hour. Then Bedivere got on his knees and lifted his king, staggering slightly beneath the dead man's weight as he stood. There was nowhere to take him, but he could not just leave him there on the field.

Bedivere carried Arthur toward the sea crashing at the bottom of tall rocky cliffs. The way down to the ocean was steep, yet Bedivere was so deeply entrenched in sorrow that he barely noticed the difficulty.

When he reached the pebble-strewn beach, Bedivere laid Arthur down while he collected drift wood and lashed together a raft with tough beach grass as rope. It would be strong enough for his purposes. He wasn't constructing a vessel that would have to last long.

When the raft was built, he laid Arthur on it and draped his own cloak over the dead man's body. He then heaped the raft with more beach grass and wood.

Bedivere had witnessed warriors from across the North Sea bury their chieftains at sea in this way, and it seemed fitting. With the edge of his sword, he struck a flinty rock but got no spark. Repeated attempts brought no fire until he switched swords and hit the rock with Excalibur's blade. A spark instantly ignited a piece of grass, quickly creating a line of flame as it spread.

Satisfied that he'd built a bonfire strong enough not to be extinguished by the ocean breeze, he pushed the raft out into the surf and watched as the tides carried the fiery vessel away from him.

The salt of his silent tears mingled with the ocean water as he stood a long time and watched the raft disappear out to sea, the flames glinting on the darkening horizon. Once the raft was finally out of sight, Bedivere returned to the beach. With no idea where to go or what to do next, he sat on the sand as a full moon rose and waves crashed onto the shore.

In his stunned state, with his mind finally free of the pressing urgency of battles and funerals, he recalled the strange thing that had happened to him in the field that day; how he'd swung his blade down upon his enemy, spraying a veil of blood before his own eyes. His heart had hammered with the effort and the relentless horror of flying body parts until he thought he could bear no more—*when suddenly he was transported out of the battle.*

Instead of flailing his sword in a fevered dervish of frenetic violence, he was suddenly lying peacefully on a sun-drenched rock. The tranquility surrounding him in this new place was so complete that the smallest sounds could be detected. A bird sang. A brook babbled and insects buzzed.

His heart-rate slowed and the warm rock soothed his tightly clenched muscles, relaxing them. He heard a woman's soft sigh, and he had the feeling that the sound had come from his own mouth. He turned, as if, all too soon, his spirit were departing the serene space, and as he looked back he saw a woman reclining on the rock.

Long, wavy copper-colored hair fanned around her incredibly delicate, breathtakingly beautiful features. A sigh escaped lips that seemed almost poised to speak. He felt a strong urge to go back and kiss them. . . .

In the next second he was once again on the bloody battlefield, sprawled on his side. Not another man stood. As he staggered to his feet, he saw Arthur, down but still moving, several feet away. He'd had the strange but certain feeling that this mysterious flight he'd somehow taken out of his body had saved his own life.

Looking down now, he ran his good hand along Excalibur, which shone in the moonlight. His mind swam as it struggled to understand all that had just happened.

Arthur, dead.

The other knights of Camelot, slain.

Surely this was the end of the world as he knew it.

CHAPTER FIVE
Eleanore the Observant

"How was *cooking* class?" Eleanore asked pointedly when Rowena returned from her supposed cooking class yet again. She noticed the forked twig caught in the hem of Rowena's cape, the half of a leaf snarled in her gorgeous hair, the dirt smudged on the back of her wrist.

And with a glance at Rowena's feet she saw that though her sister's slippers were not dirty, her ankles were.

Eleanore had long suspected that these cooking classes were a fraud, intended only to get her youngest sister out of spinning and embroidery. But the day before Rowena had actually been dirty when she returned. And now here it was again for the second day—signs that she'd somehow gone beyond the wall. Besides everything else, the girl was wet!

Rain now pelted the window of the sewing room, and it was clear from her frizzled hair and damp cloak that Rowena had been out in it!

Rowena settled on the cushions of the window seat, carefully arranging her wet cape at her side. She gazed out the window at the falling rain. It was a habit both Eleanore, the eldest, and Rowena, the youngest—just minutes younger than Ashlynn—shared, this tendency to stare longingly out the window, lost in thought.

How had she escaped the manor wall? How could she possibly have done it? Eleanore had to know.

She, herself, burned to escape from this prison of a home. She read books; she knew she was too old to be unwed. Other women were mothers long before they were as old as she already was!

Eleanore put down her embroidery hoop and crossed the room to Rowena. "Rowena, are you feeling well?" she asked softly.

Rowena shivered and turned away from the window. "Oh, you startled me," she said.

"I see that," Eleanore commented, sitting beside her on the window seat. "I asked if you were well because I noticed a distant gaze in your eyes."

Rowena straightened and seemed to force herself back from the daydream with which she'd been involved. A too bright smile formed on her lips. "I'm quite well, thank you. I was thinking about . . . cooking."

"Cooking . . ." Eleanore repeated, bristling inwardly at what she was certain was a bold-faced lie. "And how was the lesson?"

"Fine."

"What did you learn to make?"

Rowena blinked at her blankly as if she couldn't make sense of Eleanore's question. "Um . . . pheasant," she blurted after a moment.

"Did you kill it yourself?" Eleanore probed.

Rowena's nose wrinkled in an involuntary reaction of disgust. "Of course," she answered. "It was caged outside with the geese," she added. "I had to go out and get it. It struggled and almost got away. That's how I got so wet."

Eleanore observed her with a mixture of annoyance and admiration. Rowena had anticipated Eleanore's next suspicious question and answered it before it was asked. Well, Rowena would not put her off that easily. "Then why are your slippers dry though the rest of you is wet?"

"I removed them for fear of ruining them."

"Did the new kitchen servant show you how to kill the pheasant?" Eleanore pressed, undeterred.

Rowena cast a blank, uncomprehending stare at her.

"You've spent so much time in the kitchen that surely you've met Millicent, Helen's new helper," Eleanore elaborated on her question. *Ha!* she thought triumphantly as Rowena continued to stare at her with helpless incomprehension. *I've got you now!*

If she ever needed absolute proof that Rowena had not spent a single minute in the kitchen, this was it! Millicent had been helping Helen in the kitchen for more than a month now. If Rowena had been there she would have surely known that.

Rowena grasped Eleanore's hand and lowered her voice. "I have been out in the courtyard," she said. "I have found a small break in the wall, and I like to look through it."

A flood of urgency surged through Eleanore's veins. A million questions raced forward in her mind. *Had Rowena seen anyone? Had anyone seen her?*

Then she noticed, again, the small piece of leaf in Rowena's damp hair. "Are you sure you did not find a way *through* the opening?" Eleanore asked, gently extracting the leaf fragment.

Rowena took it from her. "This must have fallen inside the courtyard," she insisted. She suddenly stared intently at Eleanore. "Have you ever seen a battle?" she asked. "The kind with swords, and knights, and blood?"

Eleanore drew back, surprised by the question. "No. Did you see a battle through the wall opening?"

"It was a sort of dream," Rowena replied, her eyes troubled by the memory. "I don't think I was asleep, though I suppose it's possible that I dreamt it. It was so real, as if I was actually on the battlefield." A shudder ran through her as she appeared to relive the awful event.

Suddenly a strange glow began to emanate from beneath the velvet cape Rowena had tucked between herself and the window. Eleanore imagined a giant firefly had awoken beneath the cape. Before Rowena could stop her, she drew the cape back and beheld a beautiful bowl lined with gold. A ball of light swirled within it.

"What is it?" Eleanore demanded.

CHAPTER SIX
Rowena's Scrying Bowl

Rowena looked up at Eleanore, her mind working hard to think of a way to explain the bowl without admitting she'd been in the forest. It would be easier to tell the truth, but then all her sisters would want to go and her father would be on to them in no time.

The true story was that once again, as she had done the day before, she'd slipped through the opening in the wall and stole out into the forest under the pretense of taking a cooking class. It had been just hours ago.

The day was gray and she clutched at her cape. Taking off her slippers and stockings, she once again began to pick her way over slippery rocks and fallen branches, moss and damp dirt. A mist of rain had caused strands of hair to dampen against her forehead.

She'd gone only several steps when she paused.

An ornate bowl, from which a strange light emanated, had sat nestled in the gnarled roots of a giant, dead tree. The sky had been so gray that the unearthly swirl of light couldn't have been a reflection of the sun caught in the bowl's golden interior.

Rowena had knelt and picked up the bowl, cupping it in her hands. The light continued to swirl inside the bowl, then unexpectedly expanded until it poured out of the bowl.

Frightened, she'd tossed away the bowl, which had slid across moss before coming to rest upside down. The glow had shone a few minutes more, illuminating the mossy ground, and then receded. Wary yet curious, Rowena had retrieved the bowl, now looking simply like an elegant vessel with a golden interior.

At that moment the sky had opened, making a furious tapping on the leaves above her head. Clutching the bowl under her cape, she'd run back to the manor. Her first stop had been to her bedchamber, where she'd planned to hide the bowl in her trunk. But two maids were in there cleaning along with plump, affable Mary, who was supervising them. "We'll be done in a moment, love," she told Rowena. "Go join your sisters in the sewing room for now."

Rowena had done that, hoping to conceal the bowl under her cape. She'd meant to keep it hidden from them at least until she could think of a way to explain where she'd found it without revealing that she'd been out in the forest.

But now eleven curious faces surrounded her, alerted by Eleanore's loud question. "What is it?" asked Cecily, echoing her sister's query, unable to take her eyes off the ever-expanding ball of light in the bowl.

Staring more closely into the spinning glow, Rowena observed an image of a figure moving inside the ball of light. It was in miniature, like a small, moving painting.

Straining to bring the blurry image into focus, she saw that the figure was female. If all her sisters had not been standing around her, she might have thought the figure was one of them; the family resemblance was that strong. Could it be some twelfth sister?

The woman in the glowing ball gestured, as though she wanted to show Rowena something. Why was she so blurry, though? Was she under water? That's how it seemed to Rowena, but how could she breathe if she were underwater?

Rowena glanced up at her sisters. "What do you think she's trying to tell us?" she asked.

"Who?" Bronwyn asked.

"Don't you see the woman in the bowl?" Rowena asked.

"I only see light," Mathilde said, and the others nodded in agreement.

Looking back to the figure in the bowl, Rowena saw that the woman had lain down as if asleep. Then she stood and pointed at the floor. What was she trying to say?

With the bowl still in her hands, Rowena left the sewing chamber and headed down the wide, turning staircase toward the first floor bedchamber that all twelve girls shared. Her sisters trailed along behind her.

"What is this strange bowl, Rowena?" Chloe asked. "Where are you taking it?"

"I want to see something," Rowena replied.

They entered the bedchamber with its twelve beds, six on either side of the large room. It was each girl's favorite place in the whole manor house because it was all that remained of the original cottage before the other rooms and floors had been added. It retained the original wooden walls, rustic beams, and wide, rough-hewn floorboards.

Once they were all inside, Rowena locked the door and dropped to her knees. Flattening onto the floor, she peered under the rows of beds. Not seeing what she searched for on one side, she did the same thing on the other.

"What are you looking for?" asked Cecily.

Rowena picked herself off the floor and sat back on her heels. Glancing down, she saw that the woman in the glow was still pointing to the floor. "What do *you* see?" Eleanore asked, keenly interested.

When Rowena told her, a look of sudden inspiration swept across Eleanor's face. Hurrying to the last bed, the one in which she, herself, slept, she gestured for her sisters to assist her in shoving it away from the wall. As soon as the bed was moved, they saw a trapdoor with an iron handle in the floor.

The sisters shot questioning looks at Eleanore. "What is it?" Mathilde asked.

"I discovered it a long time ago," she explained. "A breeze wafts up from its cracks and the cold air wakes me sometimes in the night. It cools me in summer but makes me shiver in winter."

"Why have you never mentioned it before?" Ione questioned.

"It's always been there, ever since we moved into this room," Eleanore explained. "I never gave the door much thought. I assumed it was simply part of the house, an old root cellar or something. This room was originally the back part of the kitchen."

The room became alive with nervous anticipation. "You say she's pointing to the floor?" Gwendolyn checked with Rowena.

Rowena nodded.

They all looked to Eleanore as they always did in times of indecision. "Perhaps we should tell father of this," Eleanore considered.

The girls scowled at her. "This is no time to be so sensible," Rowena objected, voicing what they were all thinking. Here was an adventure thrown in their path when they were so absolutely starved for anything new and exciting.

Eleanore nodded a bit reluctantly and bent forward to grasp the handle. Tugging at it, she managed to pry it up slightly. Her sisters immediately came forward to help her, crowding their hands onto the handle.

"Now!" Eleanore shouted as they united to give the door a powerful yank. The effort threw them backward onto the floor in a pile.

As they got up, Rowena was the first to begin

moving to the drum and lute music wafting through the open trapdoor. At first she didn't even know she was swaying in time with it, but then she noticed her sisters doing the same. As if unable to resist, she stepped forward and turned in a full circle, swinging her arms in a graceful arc as she went.

The drumbeats grew louder, more insistent, moving the sisters faster and faster with their driving rhythms. The sisters laughed with giddy delight, jubilant as they twirled and leapt. The music swelled to a crashing crescendo and, one by one, the sisters climbed down into the opening in the floor.

CHAPTER SEVEN
Morgan le Fey Watches

Just before the monastery bell sounded, the field mouse finished its run across the rainy courtyard. It darted into the manor kitchen through its usual tunnel under the kitchen wall.

Helen, the cook, spotted it instantly.

"Be gone, you mouse! You pest!" Helen beat at the field mouse with the end of her straw broom. The mouse hid behind a chest and waited until a *bang* told it that Helen had gone out the back door into the rain. It quickly ran to the center of the kitchen. A flash of purple light filled the room.

A woman dressed as a servant stood where the mouse had been. Sharp features and sunken cheeks were made even more unpleasant by her beady, angry eyes. She peered around the kitchen with a look of disgust, her lip curling in dismay at her surroundings.

"Ah! Millicent! You gave me a fright!" Helen cried as she came back inside, one hand held over her head against the rain, the other holding something in her apron. "How you do pop in and out! It's not normal!"

Onto a table she emptied the damp contents of

her apron, fresh herbs from the garden: thyme, rosemary, lavender, and lemongrass. "Gather half the herbs into bundles and hang them to dry. Leave the other half for the chicken tonight."

Millicent wandered over to a bowl of fiddlehead ferns and began munching the tender shoots.

"Mind me, Millicent!" Helen scolded. "If I didn't need the help so badly I'd boot you back to wherever it is you came from."

Millicent sneered at her indolently. *If you only knew with whom you were toying,* she thought as she lazily gathered up the herbs and tossed them into her apron. She took them out into the wet courtyard letting the back door slam behind her. Letting the herbs drop onto the ground, she stepped back from the building and gazed up at the rain-soaked windows. She couldn't see Vivienne's brats, though she knew they must be up there.

Her face tightened with anger. Why hadn't she been given the gift of second sight? She, who had so many powers, could shift shape without a thought, yet she could *not* see any more than the merest of mortals! For her, a scrying pool was no more than a bucket of murky water.

Ah, but she knew Vivienne, grand mistress of second sight in every way, was trying to contact someone. She felt the increase of energy in the air, felt it in her very bones. She'd been aware of it for more than a month now. That's why she'd assumed these humiliating forms to come in and have a look.

At first, she'd thought it would be good enough to come in as a mouse. But she soon discovered that the form didn't allow her to hear what the prattling girls were saying. Their voices were like banging gongs to her in that tiny form. They hurt her large ears with their screams of laughter and endless blabber.

So she'd hit upon the idea of transforming into a servant. That way she could observe the girls and also hear the gossip of the other servants—not that there was any good gossip. How could there be with twelve girls shut up in this manor as if it were a convent?

She'd been aware, of course, that Vivienne had tried to contact them before, that she never really stopped trying. Whatever she was doing wasn't working, though. These girls seemed completely unaware of their mother's attempts to contact them.

But now things were happening.

She knew that three priestesses from the mystic island of Avalon had gone out in a golden ship to retrieve Arthur's slain body. They'd plucked him from a fiery raft and taken him back to Avalon for a proper burial.

It infuriated her! Where was the royal funeral envoy for her slain son? If she had not spirited his body away it would have lain there on the blood-soaked battlefield along with the rest, unattended and unmourned.

For Mordred, the priestesses had no time. Only precious Arthur, the *great king*, merited their attention. She and her son had disgraced the island of

Avalon, they said. They wanted nothing to do with Morgan le Fey or her son, Mordred.

Let them do as they liked. She was Morgan le Fey, the greatest sorceress the world had ever seen, and she could care for herself—more than care for herself.

Arthur was dead now, but she had learned that Excalibur was not on the burning raft with his body. Nor was it in the hands of the priestesses of Avalon. Where was it? All the soldiers and knights had died that day. Had some beggar or thief come along and taken it?

A terrible realization struck her. Vivienne must be searching for Excalibur! That was it! Even from her watery prison beneath the ground, she'd discovered—no doubt by means of her powers of second sight—what had happened to Arthur!

Morgan le Fey could not allow Vivienne to get Excalibur before she did. It might provide her with enough power to break free!

A line of worry creased Morgan's brow. That one daughter had gone roaming in the forest yesterday and again today. She didn't see what difference it could possibly make. Vivienne hadn't been able to contact them for the last twelve years. Surely it didn't matter what side of a wall they stood on.

Still, something *was* happening. And she was determined to find out what it was.

PART TWO

The Night Moves

CHAPTER EIGHT
Vivienne's Call

Vivienne was aware of the very moment she contacted her girls. She saw Rowena's green eyes in her mind with utter clarity.

The last time Vivienne had seen those eyes they belonged to a baby, but she recognized their distinct color. Even Rowena's twin sister, Ashlynn, did not have eyes that were the same clear celery green; hers were, instead, flecked with hazel.

Rowena must have somehow, through some lucky happenstance, come upon the scrying bowl at last!

Oh, and such clever girls she had! Leave it to Eleanore, always so keenly observant even as a child, to notice and recall the opening in the floor, just as Vivienne had hoped she would.

In her wild frenzy of enchanted tunneling, Vivienne had created a passageway that cut right into the root cellar under the cottage. It was a passage with a dry path that they would be able to follow all the way to the lake.

Vivienne began to pace, wishing she could see the girls. Apparently Rowena had put the bowl down, leaving it behind in the bedchamber.

She'd lost contact with them for now, but if they found her she'd require a way to signal them that she was nearby.

Gazing upward through the water, Vivienne concentrated on minerals she knew floated in the lake water. "Minerals burn with fiery might; out of watery depths glow with light!"

CHAPTER NINE
Rowena's Search

The music drew the sisters through dark passages. Time lost meaning as they traveled farther into the earth. In places, the air became moist, then dry again, then damp once more.

As they went Rowena had the feeling that they were on a quest of some kind, searching for something. Were they looking for the woman in the bowl?

They came to a dark, stony ledge running along a stone wall. The tunnel's music became faint and the urge to dance faded along with it. They had to feel their way along in the dark. Rowena was aware that the rock wall at her side was becoming wet. Soon drops of cold water fell on her nose and cheeks from the rock ceiling overhead.

In another several yards they came out to a cavern many stories high. Luminous stalagmites jutted up from the earth bathing the cavern in gentle light. Gazing upward, the sisters marveled at the spectacular stalactites, some reaching nearly to the floor. They, too, gave off a phosphorescent light.

In the center of this cavern was a wide, sparkling

lake. Tiny but sharp lights danced just below its crystal clear surface. "What are those lights?" Rowena questioned, her voice echoing off the stony walls.

She walked with her sisters to the edge of the underground lake. All twelve of them were reflected back to her in its surface. The lights appeared to dance across their hair and clothing, transforming them into magical creatures. "The lights make us look like fairies," Mathilde observed with a delighted giggle.

"Or princesses covered in diamonds," added Ashlynn.

After they had gazed at their reflections awhile longer, the girls began to settle on the many rocks in the cavern to rest. Looking around, Rowena saw that there were many entrances into the cavern. It made her wonder how extensive the network of tunnels around this cavern actually was.

Rowena sat beside Eleanore. So much had happened in these few hours just past and Rowena hardly understood any of it.

"I think the woman whom you saw in the bowl is our mother," Eleanore said after a few moments of silence.

Her words caught Rowena's breath. What Eleanore had said was so unexpected. Then she recalled how she'd noticed the resemblance. "Why do you say that?" she questioned.

"You were a baby, but I remember her gazing searchingly into a gold-lined bowl such as the one we now have," Eleanore told her.

"Why am I the only one who can see her?" Rowena asked.

Eleanore shook her head. "I don't know. I always had the feeling, though, that our mother had some kind of power, some gift for seeing beyond regular sight. Perhaps you have it too."

"Do you think our mother still lives?"

Eleanore snorted disdainfully. "What does it matter? If she's alive she's proved she doesn't care about us." As she spoke, tears welled in Eleanore's eyes, but she brushed them away brusquely. "Dead or alive, she can't do us much good so I try not to think about her."

Rowena didn't think much about her mother either because she barely remembered her. Yet the idea that she might have caught a glimpse of her in the bowl was too intriguing to dismiss. "Why would I have seen her in the bowl?" she wondered aloud.

"Perhaps the bowl holds memories," Eleanore suggested.

"I have no memory of our mother, not any clear ones," Rowena pointed out. "Sometimes I think I recall the smell of her, though. I think she smelled like lake water, although I have never seen, much less smelled, a lake. At least not until right now, and I'm not sure this is a normal lake."

"You've seen a lake before," Eleanore corrected her. "There was once a lake next to our home. Our mother let us swim in it with her all the time."

Although they couldn't see over the wall, the girls

could peer down past it from the top windows of the manor. Even if she had not gone out, Rowena would have known there was no lake in the forest. "What happened to it?" she asked.

"It disappeared at the same time our mother left. Father never mentioned it to anyone—as if it had never been there," Eleanore replied.

"Don't you think it's odd that he didn't question it?" Rowena pressed.

"The whole thing is strange," Eleanore agreed. "But isn't it strange that we are sitting in a huge cavern right now?"

Rowena smiled at Eleanore's words. "Incredibly odd, yes."

Eleanore stood abruptly as a new worry seized her. "I'm not sure we know the way back," she said glancing around at the many pathways leading into the cavern.

"We came in that way," Rowena said, pointing at the passage directly behind them.

"I think it was over there," Gwendolyn called to them.

The sisters came back together as the seriousness of their situation dawned on them. "Where's the music?" Rowena asked. "Perhaps we can follow that back."

They listened intently until they detected the faintest strains of lute music. The sisters gazed at one another hopefully before realizing that the music was coming from every opening in the cavernous rock wall.

Chapter Ten
Sir Bedivere No More

Sir Bedivere began walking along the shore, heedless of the effects of the surf on his chain mail armor. He had secured Excalibur in his own scabbard and tucked his sword into his belt. With no thought to a destination, he moved like a sleepwalker. When hunger gripped his stomach, he barely noticed it.

So deep and complete was his despair that he remained nearly oblivious to the pounding surf or the calling seabirds overhead. He was the walking dead, the last man standing in a battle that had taken every last soul.

He would have walked into the ocean, confident that his heavy armor would weigh him down beneath its waves, if it had not been for his promise to the dying Arthur. Now he was obliged to stay alive long enough to fulfill his mission—and not a moment longer.

Would any lake do for completing the task? Did he have to throw the sword into a special lake? How would he ever know if he'd done it right? Why do it at all? Arthur was dead—what difference could this make to him now?

Still, he had sworn. He'd given his word as a knight of the Round Table. The importance of that might be fast becoming a memory, disappearing from the world altogether, but it was still crucial to him.

Arthur had taken him on as a groom and valet when he was but twelve and Arthur was a young king. Bedivere had carried Arthur's armor, readied his clothing, made sure his horse was watered and brushed down properly. The servant had grown to be a companion, confidant, and—in his early teen years, when Arthur felt he'd earned it—knight.

In the five years he'd been a knight he had seen and done unimaginable things. He'd helped Arthur do battle with a village of mountain people, all closely related to one another, who were so big— both tall and wide—that they were considered giants by their neighbors.

When these giants began kidnapping young women from neighboring towns, desiring to bring new bloodlines into their gigantic genes, the towns-people prevailed on Arthur and Bedivere to save their captured wives and daughters. They'd returned every last woman, though the giants had left the warriors battered and in need of new armor.

He had been beside Arthur when they slew a fierce cave-dwelling creature with breath so hot people claimed it breathed fire. Merlin had looked it up in his volume of ancient wisdom and identified it as a pterosaur, though the terrified local villagers had named it a dragon.

When Arthur wed his queen, Guinevere, and began staying closer to Camelot, Bedivere had still believed that their days of adventure, merriment, and chivalry would go on forever. Even after he'd lost the use of his left hand while fighting beside Arthur against the Saxon invaders, he'd remained hopeful. He never would have believed that such a defeat as they had just suffered would ever come to them. But now he was certain that a new age of darkness had befallen.

He stopped only to sleep on the sand. That night he woke up with the high tide nearly over his mouth and scrambled up to higher ground to resume his slumber. At dawn he awoke again to find sand and pebbles covering him. It scratched him so badly that he shed his armor until he was down to his tunic, leggings, and boots. The only piece he retained was his belt with its scabbard containing Excalibur and his own sword.

By the time Bedivere staggered off the shoreline and into Glastonbury he looked every bit the wild madman he felt himself to be.

"Hey, you, one hand!" a richly dressed man called to him as he withdrew a fat purse from beneath his cape. "How much will you take for the sword?"

Bedivere's eyes darted to his lame hand. When he was in full armor he could conceal its condition under a sleeve of chain mail, but now it was exposed for the useless appendage it had become. Stung by the humiliating insult, he glowered at the man.

"Oh come now," the man cajoled. "You must have

stolen it from some very grand fallen knight. There are quite a few of them these days I hear tell. It can be of no use to you, but my gold coins might buy you a meal—or a bath!" Chuckling at his own words, the man poured out several coins and advanced to Bedivere, his hand offering the coins.

Slowly Bedivere withdrew Excalibur from his scabbard.

"There's a bright fellow," the man said, misunderstanding Bedivere's intention.

Bedivere slashed the sword over the man's head with the lightning movement he was known for. Dropping his coins, the man fled, horrified.

Giggles and applause made Bedivere turn. Two dirty, ragged children sat on a stone curb, pleased by the display. Bedivere scooped up the dropped coins and tossed them gently in their direction. "We know where there's a spare straw mat in beggar's alley, but you have to be fast to get it," one of the children, a girl of about six told Bedivere as she stuck one of the coins into the pocket of her skirt.

"Yeah, the old man who had it died last night," added a boy of about seven. "If you hurry I think the mat is still there."

With a nod of consent, Bedivere followed the excited children into the poorest part of the town. He learned that the boy was named Amren and the girl was Evanola. They led him down a narrow alley where beggars were living. "You're in luck," said Evanola. "Here's the mat!"

"We can come back with a piece of potato for you later," Amren offered. "Mum used to have me bring it to the old man, and I don't think she knows he's dead yet. I'll give it to you."

"How'd you hurt your hand?" Evanola asked staring at the coarse scar running across his palm.

"In a fight," Bedivere replied as he settled onto the moldy mat.

"We'll be back with that piece of potato, don't you worry," Amren assured him as he and his sister ran off.

Bedivere waved to them languidly as he turned on his side and took his place among the beggars in the alleyway.

CHAPTER ELEVEN
Eleanore's Earring

If Eleanore did not get out of this darkness soon, she would go mad! She was sure of it. How long had they been wandering in these twisting, turning tunnels?

It would be the fault of her parents if she did lose her mind. Her mother, going off and abandoning them, then suddenly appearing, years later, in some sort of a bowl—of all things!

It *was* their mother that Rowena had seen; she had no doubt of it. She and Mathilde were the ones who remembered her best, being the oldest. They all looked like her in one way or another.

Their father was to blame too. Locking them inside like prisoners! Making them so desperate to escape that they'd scramble into a tunnel with no heed for where they were going or where they might end up! And now they were lost—hopelessly lost in the dark.

Something scrambled by her foot and Eleanore jumped back. "Careful!" cried Isolde who was right behind her. "You nearly knocked me down."

"I've caught a mouse," said Ione, who was never squeamish about such things. "It ran across my slipper and I grabbed it."

"Hold on to it," Eleanore said to her. Groping her way forward past her other sisters, she came to Ione. Her eyes had adjusted to the darkness well enough to let her see Ione and the mouse a little. Bending, she pulled the ribbon from the lavender silk slippers she wore. She removed her earring and fastened it to the ribbon, and then she tied the ribbon around the end of the mouse's tail. "Now let it go," she instructed her sister.

Just as she'd hoped, the earring clattered as the mouse scurried away ahead of them. "Come on, hurry, while we can still hear it," she told her sisters. They followed the sound, as quickly as they could go, and it wasn't long before they saw a dim light in the distance—it was the trapdoor opening.

They climbed back into their bedchamber just as there came an urgent pounding on the door. "Yes," cried Eleanore, reaching to pull Bronwyn through the opening.

Bronwyn, in turn, helped pull the next sister, Isolde, through while Eleanore opened the door a crack. On the other side was short, plump Mary, the head housekeeper. "Thank goodness," she cried when she saw Eleanore.

She was about to come in but Eleanore blocked her way. She needed to give her sisters time to shove the bed back over the trapdoor. "Is there something you need?" she asked Mary.

"Something I need?" Mary cried incredulously. "I've been pounding on that locked door since supper. Where have you girls been?" Red splotches formed on her cheeks as she pushed past Eleanore.

The sisters had managed to get the bed back into place and had piled onto it as if to further cover the opening with their long dresses. "We've been right here," Eleanore told her.

"You have not been!" Mary scolded. "When I called you to eat there was no one in here. I heard not a sound! You may thank me for I told your father that you were all feeling ill being that it was your time of month."

"All of us at once?" Cecily questioned, raising a skeptical brow.

"It happens among females who live in close quarters: Their cycles become attuned to one another," Mary maintained. "Besides, I had to say *something*. I didn't want to worry the poor man. Now I must know the truth! Where have you been?"

"We've been right here," Eleanore insisted once again.

Mary pointed an accusing finger at the eleven pairs of dirty, tattered silk slippers dangling from the bed just above the floor. "And your slippers got into that sorry state because you have been here in your room all the while, I suppose!"

"We were dancing," Eleanore said.

"What? In a dust bin?" Mary demanded.

The sisters glanced at one another. How could they explain the disastrous state of their slippers?

They couldn't. So they stared at Mary, dumbfounded but unwilling to reveal their secret. After a long, uncomfortable moment Mary breathed a sigh of resignation. "It's very late and I have not gotten any sleep. Give me those slippers. In the morning I'll discard them and bring you new ones from the storage chest."

The sisters removed their slippers and handed them to her. "Look at these expensive slippers— ruined! Your father would get into a state if he saw these," Mary muttered crossly as she collected them in her outstretched skirt.

"What are you going to do with them?" Rowena asked as she bent to pull off her slippers.

"I don't know—burn them before your father sees them I imagine," Mary replied as Rowena dropped them into her apron. "There are replacements in the storage cabinet, but I know he would not be pleased. These shoes are not a month old." Mary scowled at the sisters, encompassing them all in a sweeping glare of disapproval, before leaving with the slippers.

When the door closed behind Mary, Eleanore was suddenly extremely tired. Rowena had wandered to the window and was gazing dreamily out into the night. The other ten had fallen asleep where they lay, bundled in a heap on her bed.

Stretching wearily, Eleanore laid down on an empty bed and her eyes began to close. Just as she was about to fall asleep, a familiar noise brought her back to waking.

The mouse that had guided them out of the passage scurried along a floor board, her earring still attached to the ribbon tied to its tail. The mouse stopped and regarded her, its pink nose twitching.

She rose off her pillow and considered attempting to get her earring back. But she'd need Ione's help for that and it appeared that she was already sleeping. Just then Eleanore desperately needed to sleep, as well. She lay her head back on the pillow and allowed the mouse to continue on its way, still bouncing the earring off the floorboards as it departed the room.

CHAPTER TWELVE
Sir Ethan's Outrage

"Stop right now!" Sir Ethan's authoritative voice boomed in the kitchen hallway.

Mary froze in front of the blazing fireplace with her arms wrapped around a straw basket containing twenty-three tattered, jewel-toned, ribbon-trimmed, silk slippers. Though it was barely dawn, she'd only had the chance to pitch one slipper into the flames before Sir Ethan appeared.

"Why are these slippers going into the fire?" he demanded to know.

Mary tried her best to smile casually at him. "Oh, they've simply been worn out," she said as if it were quite normal.

"Worn out?" he questioned, lifting one of the slippers from the basket and turning it in his hand. "These floors are polished marble, and the courtyard is covered in slate. How could they be wearing their slippers out so quickly on such smooth surfaces?" He ran his other hand along the scuffed, torn, dirty sole of the slipper he held, and his eyes narrowed suspiciously.

This slipper had obviously been worn outside over some kind of rocky surface. Apparently all the slippers had been worn outdoors, judging from the sight of them. He was not a fool. "Tell me, Mary. Last night when you told me that the girls were . . . indisposed . . . and could not come to supper, are you sure they were actually in their room?"

Mary was not naturally inclined to lie, and at the moment it seemed fruitless to try. Her master was clearly on the trail of the truth. "I did not *see* them exactly," she admitted sheepishly. "I simply *assumed* they were within and felt it likely that they might be down with womanly ills when they did not answer my call to dine."

Sir Ethan harrumphed unhappily. "I see. And were these slippers in such disrepair yesterday?"

"I could not tell you," Mary replied.

Sir Ethan took the basket of slippers from Mary and headed out of the kitchen, striding purposefully to the bedchamber his daughters shared. He pounded forcefully on the door. "It is your father, open up," he bellowed. When he got no reply, he banged on the door even louder.

Still no reply came. Cracking open the unlocked door, he peered in.

Ten of his daughters were asleep on one bed, heaped on one another in a tangle of arms and legs. Eleanore was sprawled on another bed, in such a sound sleep that she snored. And Rowena slumbered on the floor, slumped against the wall below the bedroom window.

Not one of them wore a nightgown; all were still

fully clothed for daytime. "They look like a pack of drunken revelers passed out after a night of riotous merriment," he said to Mary, who had hurried into the room and now stood beside him wringing her hands anxiously.

She stepped beside Rowena and attempted to jostle her awake, but the young woman simply murmured incoherently and repositioned herself on the floor. "Let her be," Sir Ethan told Mary.

He left the room with Mary at his side. "Issue a new pair of slippers to each girl. Every morning the slippers are to be lined up outside this bedchamber for my inspection. In that manner I will quickly get to the bottom of whatever is going on with them."

"I'm sure it's nothing of great concern," Mary said.

Sir Ethan was *not* as sure. If his daughters were going out into the world through some route he did not know, any manner of harm could come to them. He would not have it and could not even bear the thought of it.

"I'm going into town," he told Mary abruptly. "I will return with the locksmith and have him fit the entire manor with new, stronger locks. The bolt on the girls' door will be the first to be changed. No longer will it lock from within, but rather every night you will be charged with the duty of bolting it from the outside."

"As you wish, sir," Mary said as he dashed away toward the front door.

Chapter Thirteen
Rowena Meets Millicent

The boy who tended the geese in the yard always left his muddy dung-caked boots outside the kitchen door, so Rowena was confident they'd be there when she came to find them. With a quick check to see if she was being observed, she lifted her hem and slipped her stocking feet into them—a nearly perfect fit.

She had arisen an hour earlier, stiff limbed from sleeping on the cold floor, and looked outside just in time to see the boy pass through the front gate with her father, who had no doubt recruited the servant to attend him on some errand in Glastonbury. It would be hours before he had need of these rough boots again. But she needed them.

She had awoken to find her only footwear, her slippers, gone. Then she recalled that she'd given them to Mary for burning. No replacements had yet been delivered to the room. On the previous days she'd found it difficult to walk barefoot through the rocks and sticks, which was why she hoped to borrow these boots for today's trip into the forest.

"Going somewhere?"

Looking up sharply, Rowena faced the woman

who had spoken. She'd never seen her before, and as she took in the sharp features, sunken cheeks, and beady, peering eyes, her first impression was overwhelmingly negative.

The woman offered her something small and glittering, holding it out in the palm of her hand. "I found this," she said, and Rowena saw she held Eleanore's earring. "I've just started here, and I don't want to be accused of stealing. Take it."

Rowena plucked it from her hand, inwardly recoiling at the touch of the woman's cold palm. "Thank you," she said as she recovered from her initial revulsion. She remembered that Eleanore had told her there was a new kitchen servant, Millicent. Rowena assumed this was she.

"Where are you headed in the goose boy's boots?" the woman asked with a swaggering insolence and hint of menace that put Rowena further on her guard.

Rowena forced a smile. "Where is there to go?"

Millicent responded with a tight, joyless grin and nodded toward the boots.

"Millicent!" Helen shouted from inside the kitchen. "Where have you disappeared to now?"

Millicent's eyes darted toward the kitchen door, but she made no move to go as she stubbornly awaited Rowena's answer.

"I was simply wondering what they felt like," Rowena told her, stepping out of them.

"Millicent!" Helen shouted again, this time in a more exasperated tone.

Millicent reluctantly moved toward the kitchen door. Rowena snapped up the boots and thrust them at her as she opened the door. "These need to be cleaned," she said in her most imperious tone.

She did not want this woman with her bullying manner to think she was afraid of her. And she needed to prove that she did not intend to go anywhere wearing the goose boy's boots.

With a hate-filled glower, the woman took them from her and went inside.

Rowena glanced at Eleanore's earring and put it in the pocket of her gown. She no longer felt sure it was a wise idea to go out into the forest as she'd intended. Was Millicent watching her? She struck Rowena as the kind of angry, resentful person who might delight in causing trouble for her.

But the trees were swept by the spring breezes and rustled above the manor wall. Her sisters were asleep; her father was out. If Millicent had not delayed her she'd be in the forest now.

Glancing in the kitchen window, she saw Millicent fiercely plucking the feathers from a chicken while Helen pounded and kneaded a mound of bread dough. Mary led two servant boys into the kitchen and put a pile of cutting utensils before them for sharpening on a stone.

Rowena rolled off her stockings and padded across the slate courtyard in bare feet. She was quickly through the opening she'd made in the wall and once again wandering through the forest.

There was so much she wanted to think about. Everything that had happened in the past days was so confusing. Who was the mysterious soldier who had touched her heart so profoundly? Did he even exist? Had he died in that battle? Why had she seen him, even changed places with him?

The thought that he might be dead made her shiver, and she cast it aside. She had already fallen so deeply and inexplicably in love with him that the idea of his death was too terrible to be considered for even a moment.

And what of the bowl she'd found and the trip into the underground cavern that had followed? Was Eleanore correct—was the figure in the bowl really their mother? If so, what was she trying to convey to them?

Rowena came upon the boulder she'd rested on the first day she came out into the forest, the one on which she'd had her vision of the battlefield. If she sat on it again, would she once more see the face of her beautiful knight?

Stretching out on the boulder, she rested her cheek on its sun-drenched surface. Its heat soothed the scratches on her forest-roughened feet.

She closed her eyes letting the sunlight create sparks of color behind her lids. Soon the colors formed patterns, falling into place like a puzzle.

And then she was in another part of the forest. She was coming off a road. She felt such inner heaviness, such despair within her. She knew she was no longer in her own body;

surely she had never known this kind of hopeless sadness.

In the next moment, something ethereal inside her lifted up and was able to look down. It was her knight, no longer in armor, looking like the poorest of beggars—but she recognized him just the same.

And yet, he was so different!

Now that she saw him without his helmet, she found him to be even more handsome than she had thought. But a scruffy growth of beard now covered his chin and cheeks, and his face had grown gaunt.

In this vision he was moving through a forest much like the one she was in—coming closer at every moment.

CHAPTER FOURTEEN
Bedivere's Fight

Bedivere wanted nothing more than to rid himself of Excalibur. During the time he'd slept on the old dead beggar's mat, he'd twice had to leap up to thwart thieves trying to lift it from his scabbard.

He could hardly blame the would-be robbers. Even *he* had considered keeping Arthur's grand, enchanted sword for himself. Its workmanship was like none other, and the jewels on its hilt made it worth a fortune. And then there was the matter of its enchantment. He'd often seen Arthur bloodied in battle only to be miraculously healed. The lethal blow Mordred had dealt him had to have occurred because of some exceptionally strong dark magic.

For its great value, its sentimental worth, and its magic, Bedivere longed to keep Excalibur and was sorely tempted to do so. *But I am a knight of the Round Table*, he reminded himself at the times when his desire to possess the sword threatened to overwhelm him. Although he now lived in a world that might scoff at his idealism, his high standards regarding honor and duty, it still meant everything to him. The code of the Round Table defined who he was in his own mind. It didn't matter how low his fortunes fell or how demoralized he became—he would forever retain the values of a knight of the Round Table. And, as such, he could not keep his king's sword if he had promised to return it to this Lady of the Lake.

After the second thief had attacked him, just before dawn, he had been unable to fall back to sleep. His stomach rumbled with hunger, even though the boy, Amren, had been true to his promise and had come back to give him the piece of potato.

He walked out of the still-sleeping town, heading down a road in search of a lake, or at least some information about the Lady of the Lake. Just as the sky was nearly light, he'd come to a monastery and knocked on the door.

The old monk who answered, Brother Louis, understandably mistook Bedivere for a beggar looking for a meal and ushered him into the monastery's plain kitchen with its long wooden tables and huge fireplace. The breakfast of freshly laid eggs and newly baked bread went a long way toward restoring Bedivere's strength.

"Do you know where I might find either the Lady of the Lake or her special lake?" Bedivere inquired of Brother Louis, who had sat down beside him as he swallowed the last of his bread.

"The followers of the old ways spoke of this lady," the monk said with a serious expression. "It is said that she was close to Merlin, adviser to the king, and is herself a powerful sorceress."

Bedivere had met Merlin, the ancient sorcerer, many times. He would have sought out his advice on this matter, but the old wizard had disappeared just months before the battle at Camlan. "Do you know where I might find the lake where this lady dwells?" Bedivere pressed the monk.

Brother Louis grew reluctant to talk about the subject. He tried to convince Bedivere that the world of enchanters, sorcerers, and spirits was best avoided. "You may stay here with us, if you wish," he offered. "A monk's life is simple, but it is holy."

Bedivere was tempted to follow the monk's advice. "I may, someday, do that very thing," he said sincerely, "for I am heartsick and weary of the world. I've lost my desire for adventure, riches, fame . . . and even love. The idea of hiding away from the world in a peaceful life of prayer and service is immensely appealing to me."

"Do it, then," Brother Louis urged him.

Bedivere shook his head as he rose from the table. "I am duty-bound to perform a task, and to accomplish it, I must locate this lake."

"There is only one lake that I have ever seen in this whole area. I stumbled upon it more than twenty years ago when I was lost deep in the forest on the other side of the road. Somehow I had wandered off the road, as if under the spell of some forest spirit, and could not find my way back. It was with great relief that I came to a rustic cottage beside a glistening lake."

"A lake, you say?" Bedivere noted keenly.

Brother Louis nodded and continued. "When I knocked on the door, a gentleman with a military bearing prevailed upon me to perform a wedding ceremony. He was there with a woman of unearthly beauty, and I quickly sped through their vows and pronounced them husband and wife. No sooner had I finished the ceremony than a veil lifted from my mind and I knew clearly how to find my way out of the forest."

"And where might I find this lake beside the cottage?" Bedivere asked.

"If you continue down this road, you will come to a trail leading into the forest, though it's a hike of several hours," he said. "I hear the road was made by Sir Ethan of Colchester, but I have not actually seen it myself as I have not left the monastery since that day I lost my way so many years ago."

Bedivere thanked the old monk and headed on down the road. In several hours, he came to an area where it seemed that encampments had once been made and that a wide trail had been cut into the forest. Turning into it, he marveled at the dense foliage of this primeval forest. He could well believe that a magical lake existed in such a place.

He had walked for several miles when he climbed up a hill. When he got to the top, he gazed down at an unexpected sight.

He'd been searching for a rustic cottage and so hadn't anticipated coming upon a grand, walled manor house standing by itself in the depths of this forest. Surely this was not the place the monk had told him of. It was no mere cottage, and there was no lake to be seen.

He left the trail that led directly to the manor's wrought-iron gate and thrashed his way through the forest underbrush, assuming that the cottage and lake the monk had told him of must be farther on.

He spotted a field mouse running alongside him and birds flitting through the trees. From somewhere, he heard a brook babbling. He was overcome with the sensation that he had been in the very same place where he now stood, although he knew it was impossible; he had never been in this part of the country before.

And then he experienced that same lifting sensation he'd had at Camlan, the sense of rising out of his body and entering another.

Once again, he was on that same rock with the soothing sun washing over him.

He rose again and was able to see where he had been. It was the young woman from the day of the battle, still breathtakingly beautiful as she lay serenely on the boulder. Again he felt a strong urge to kiss her, despite the fact that to kiss a sleeping woman would have been counter to the code of chivalry by which he lived.

He was not inexperienced when it came to romantic matters. Females of all ages had always fancied him in that way. But he had never experienced anything like the tender thrill he felt when he saw her, the strong pull to embrace and kiss her.

When he fully returned to himself, walking through the forest once more, he became lost in thought, trying to imagine who this woman might be and why the sight of her filled him with such excitement. He was trying to recall every feature of her face when he was suddenly lifted off his feet by a thumping, painful blow to his back.

Landing on his chest, he pushed up and instinctively pulled Excalibur from his scabbard. He stood with the sword drawn, balanced on the balls of his feet, and prepared to fight.

A soldier made of rocks and boulders stood in front of him. Bedivere had heard of spirits who often took the form of rocks and trees. This had to be one of those.

Facing it, he swung his sword at it. The rock soldier dodged the blow, swaying to the left. Bedivere slashed at it again, and the rock soldier moved right. It then swung its stony arms forward, lifting Bedivere off the ground and hurling him into the trunk of a tree.

Excalibur flew out of his hand and lay yards away from his crippled hand, and he couldn't get to it. The rock soldier bent low and pounded him with a thick stone arm. He came down on Bedivere again, aiming to crush his head. Bedivere rolled away, but not before gashing his forehead on the rock soldier's hard stony arms.

Recovering himself, Bedivere rose and lunged for Excalibur just as the rock soldier swooped down to seize it. Bedivere got there seconds ahead and

gripped the sword. He began to hack at the rock soldier, blinded though he was by blood running from
the gash in his forehead.

The moment Excalibur clanged against the rock,
the soldier shook as though the sword's blade had
dealt it a shot of lightning.

Bedivere jumped back and watched it crumble as
it deteriorated into a pile of rubble.

He looked sharply in every direction, waiting for
another magic attack. Who knew what innocent-
looking object might suddenly spring to life in such
a place?

His knight's keen instincts told him something
had moved from behind a nearby boulder. Another
rock soldier? Even now, something was watching
him. His every nerve was alert as he slowly edged
nearer to the rock.

With a powerful leap, he sprang onto the flat
boulder, quickly shifting Excalibur so that it was
gripped between his left arm and his side, and
grabbed whatever was behind the boulder with his
good hand. His fingers clutched a handful of thick
hair, and he lifted its owner up to face him.

When he saw his captive, he drew a stunned
breath and released the lovely, young, green-eyed
woman he held.

CHAPTER FIFTEEN
Rowena

Was this another vision? The scene Rowena had just witnessed was so unbelievable—what else could it be? Surely her mystery knight was not actually there at that very moment, staring down at her with an expression of complete amazement.

"Are you a witch?" he demanded gruffly, shifting Excalibur back into his good hand.

"I could not say," Rowena answered truthfully. Up until the other day she would have been sure that she was no such thing; she might even have taken offense at the question. But these visions of him combined with her ability to see into the strange bowl had made her wonder about herself.

"If I am a witch," she added, "I mean you no harm."

"Then you did not send that soldier made of rocks to attack me?"

"Never!" she cried. "That was truly frightening. This forest is full of strangeness."

"And you are not a part of the strangeness?" he asked warily.

"The first I knew of any strange power in me was when I saw you in battle."

He backed up in surprise. She knew from his stunned expression that he understood—even if he could not quite believe it—what she was talking about. He studied her face as if deciding if he trusted her.

"I saw you, as well," he told her after a moment.

She smiled at him, appreciating his honesty. "Then are *you* a wizard?" she asked, teasing.

"Can't you see that I am a beggar?" he countered.

"A wizard might disguise himself as a beggar . . . or as a knight. It does not answer my question," she replied.

He relaxed and loosened his grip on the extravagantly jeweled sword that he held. "I am not a wizard. I have no explanation for why we seem so connected in this strange way."

"Neither have I," she said as she sat on the boulder.

Replacing his sword, he sat beside her.

"What is your name?" she asked him.

"Bedivere," he answered. "But my sisters called me Bedwyr. It's the way they say it in the North Country, where I was raised."

"Were you close to your sisters?" Rowena asked, sensing that he wanted to tell her about them.

"We used to play for hours in the hills by our home."

"What was your favorite game?" she asked.

He smiled as he recalled his boyhood. "What I loved to do with them more than anything else was dance. They taught me their folk dances." He laughed in a self-deprecating way. "They told me I was the best dancer in all the hill country."

"Are you?" she asked.

"I don't know," he answered lightly. "I have not danced in a long, long time. Of course I've partnered ladies at balls and the like, but I haven't really kicked my heels in the air since those carefree days."

They sat side by side without speaking for a moment. "Your face is bloodied from your fight," she observed after a while. She pushed the hair from his forehead. "But I cannot see where you were injured."

He touched his temple. "It's true," he murmured. "The sword I hold is said to heal the wounds of its bearer."

"It's healed your wound then," Rowena surmised.

"It appears so." His expression darkened as some unhappy thought came upon him. "Though when fighting against enchanted foes it cannot be relied on."

"What are you saying?"

He revealed to her that he held the great Excalibur and told her the story of how he had been entrusted to return it to the Lady of the Lake. Rowena excitedly told him what Eleanore had said to her just a day earlier—about the lake that had once been there. "It seems to me," she added, "that if the lake were still here, this is where it would be located."

"How could a lake disappear?" he asked.

Rowena shook her head, having no idea.

A sudden neighing of horses made them both

whirl toward the sound. "My father!" Rowena said, gasping. "Hide!"

Bedivere resisted her command, seeming to feel hiding was unmanly. "No. I'll explain to—"

She grabbed his tunic and yanked him down behind the boulder beside her. They watched together as her father, the goose boy, and another man Rowena did not recognize headed toward the manor house. The third man's appearance made Rowena think he must be some sort of artisan.

"I'd better return home," Rowena said. "He sometimes wishes to see my sisters and me after he returns from a trip away, even if he's only been gone for a few hours. If he suspects that I am missing, he will question me until he learns that I have been out in the forest."

"And then I would have no chance of ever seeing you again," Bedivere realized.

"Not in the flesh, like this," she answered as she began to rise cautiously. Her foot slid on a stone and she fell backward slightly. He reached out to steady her, wrapping his left arm around her shoulder. She noticed the odd immobility of his hand as it touched her shoulder and looked at him with a questioning expression.

"A battle wound," he explained succinctly, averting his eyes in shame.

She observed the raised, twisted scar that ran across his palm. Filled with tender compassion for his injury, she reached across herself and pressed her hand into his crippled hand.

He turned back to her suddenly and swept her up with his right arm and kissed her passionately. She returned his kiss with equal fire.

From inside the courtyard, a door slammed forcefully.

"Rowena!" her father bellowed.

Rowena sprang away from Bedivere. "I have to go. He cannot find me out here!"

"Meet me again tomorrow," he pleaded. "Right here."

"I will," she promised as she ran back toward the wall.

When she got to the wall, she pressed her back against it, trying to get some sense of where in the courtyard her father stood. She didn't hear anyone walking. Perhaps he'd gone back inside.

Her mind was racing. If she was lucky and fast, she could bolt across the courtyard and through the kitchen door. From there she could take the back staircase up to the sewing room and say she'd been there the entire time.

Kneeling first, she dropped flat to the ground and rolled to her side. She stuck her bare feet through the opening. Then, pulling the folds of her gown tightly around her body, she wiggled the rest of the way through.

As her shoulders and head came into the courtyard, she instantly became aware of her father's boots. Stiffening with anxiety, she slowly dared to look up only to see that her father was glowering down at her, his face red with fury.

Gripping Rowena under her arm, Sir Ethan yanked her roughly to standing. "Now I see how you girls have been escaping," he yelled. "Are all your sisters cavorting in the forest at this moment?"

"They don't know about the opening," Rowena spoke with a quavering voice. "I'm the only one who has gone out this way."

Sir Ethan let her drop out of his grasp. "Do not lie to me. I saw your slippers this morning. All of you have been out."

"No, truly," she insisted, "it's just me." Intimidated as she felt, she would not tell him about their adventure underground. She couldn't presume to make that decision for all of them.

"I have returned from town with a locksmith who will fit every door with a sturdy bolt," he said. "Tomorrow I will hire a mason to repair this wall. This will put an end to these adventures."

He began to storm toward the manor and Rowena trailed after him, finding her nerve once again. "Father, why do you keep us locked up like this? Would it hurt if we went into town occasionally? Might we have a party sometime? If we could see the world and meet others we might not feel so desperate to go out."

"You have books, you have instruments, beautiful clothes, fine foods," he replied. "The world holds nothing that you lack."

She stayed with him as he strode in the front door and headed toward the bedchamber the sisters shared. "We are not little girls, Father," she pointed out boldly. "I am almost of the age to be a wife—and I am your youngest daughter!"

These last words stopped him. He regarded her as if seeing her for the first time. "Perhaps it *is* time that I begin to seek suitable matches for you girls," he said with thoughtful deliberation.

Suitable matches?

Now what had she done?

She panicked as alarming images of balding, bejeweled dukes and portly merchants in fur-trimmed robes formed in her head. "Wouldn't it be better if we could meet young men we might grow to love," she suggested.

Her words seemed to awaken a disturbing memory within him. "To marry for love is foolishness. No good can come of it," he snapped, resuming his walk toward the bedchamber.

She wanted to point out that he had married for love and the twelve children he so wanted to protect had come from that union. But there was an ominous darkness in his expression, and he was so angry that it didn't seem wise to press him any further on the subject.

He reached the bedchamber where the locksmith was installing an iron bolt to the outside of the door. "What?" Rowena exclaimed when she realized he meant to lock them in their room from the outside.

She followed him into the room where her sisters still appeared sleepy-eyed, though they were awake.

Mary was there, too, distributing new slippers from a straw basket to each sister.

"Here is how it will be from now on," he announced to his daughters. "Every morning Mary will open the door and you will line these new slippers up outside the room for my inspection. She will then return the slippers to you and escort you girls to the sewing room. There, servants will bring you your meals except for supper, which you will take with me in the dining hall."

"It's as if we are in a prison!" Eleanore objected.

Sir Ethan shot her a severe, warning glance. "You are being kept safe." Whirling back toward the door, Sir Ethan departed.

"This is your fault!" Eleanore confronted Rowena. "I know you have been going out. You were just out now, weren't you? He caught you, didn't he?"

Rowena dropped her head as tears brimmed in her eyes. This was so awful—trapped like a bird in a cage, held more tightly than ever, just when the world had seemed to be opening as never before, in the very same hour in which love had come to her.

"Leave your sister alone," Mary scolded Eleanore as she walked toward the door. "Your father caught me trying to burn your ruined slippers. That's why he's on this rampage."

"And he also caught me coming in from the forest," Rowena murmured, her head still hung. The opening she'd worked on so hard and so long—that was gone now too, all those hours wasted.

"Does father think we were all in the forest?" Brianna asked.

"I told him it wasn't so, but that's what he thinks," Rowena admitted.

"Then he doesn't know anything about the opening in the floor?" Helewise mentioned.

Rowena shook her head.

"Caverns sometimes lead to the surface," Eleanore said. "I recall a romantic book from France I once read where the lovers escaped an evil sorcerer by running into a cavern. If there was a way in, there was a way out."

"So you're saying that we might still be able to find a way to get out of here by traveling through the tunnels," Chloe said excitedly.

Eleanore glanced at the closed bedchamber door. As she turned, they could hear the new bolt clanking shut. Together, the sisters scowled at the locksmith they knew was on the other side.

"It doesn't matter," Eleanore assured them. "I believe that the figure Rowena saw in the bowl was our mother." This news was greeted by a wave of murmuring, some of it excited, some disbelieving. Eleanore shushed them and continued. "If she still lives, it's up to us to find her. I've always been angry because I believed she abandoned us, but if she is in trouble we must go to her."

"Do you think it's possible that she is alive?" Helewise questioned.

"Anything is possible," Eleanore replied. "But if

she is in the next life and comes to us as a spirit, then we still owe it to her to uncover her intention in contacting us."

"But the tunnels are dark," Cecily reminded them with a shiver in her voice. "If it hadn't been for that mouse, we might be in there still."

Rowena reached in her pocket, remembering the earring Millicent had handed her. "The new servant found this and gave it to me," she told Eleanore, handing it to her.

Eleanore took it from her. "What did you think of her?"

"Unpleasant."

Eleanore nodded and then turned back to Cecily. "We will carry lamps next time," Eleanore told her. "As long as we bring enough oil, we will have light."

The sisters began to plan their next descent into the tunnels, but Rowena couldn't keep her mind on the discussion. Instead she gazed out the window at the courtyard bathed in the soft light of an early spring evening. The goose boy had once again put on his now-clean boots and was stretched on a mat in front of the opening. No doubt Sir Ethan had stationed him there to guard it.

Where was her Bedivere now? She saw again his beautiful face in her memory, once again felt his kiss. Her eyes closed as she recalled the sweetness and warmth of it. She relived the feel of his arm enfolding her, and saw anew his crippled hand with its twisting scar. Even in its ugliness, it made him dearer to her. She winced to think of the pain he had felt when it happened, and somehow she understood the humiliation it caused him now.

He wanted to meet her in the forest tomorrow. He would be there, but she would not. Would he think she did not care to come to him? The thought of him misunderstanding formed a knot that tightened painfully in her stomach. This was an unbearable torment. How would she go on if she could never see him again? She simply could not endure life without the possibility of seeing him.

"Rowena!"

Her sisters were all looking at her. "Pay attention please! We're going down through the trapdoor again tonight," Eleanore told her. "Tonight after supper we're going to try to sneak an extra lamp or two out of the dining hall. The small lamps at the tables by the doors might suit perfectly. Each of us will wear a shawl to supper so that we might hide a lamp under it."

Rowena nodded. The idea of going into the tunnels was no longer as thrilling as it had once been. All that mattered now was Bedivere, her beautiful love from the North Country.

CHAPTER SIXTEEN
Morgan Follows

Morgan chortled in delight as she sliced bread for the night's supper. She still was not exactly sure what was going on and, it was true, she had suffered a few setbacks, but, all in all, things seemed to be rolling her way.

Imagine—Vivienne suddenly appearing like that in a scrying bowl after all this time! Well, realistically, she'd probably been attempting it for years. There simply had been no one on the other end to receive her signal. But her patience had paid off at last. That Rowena had chipped her way out of the egg, eager little chick that she was, and come upon her mother's precious bowl, which apparently had been sitting right where Vivienne had left it.

Such clever girls, she thought as she placed the bread on a carved wooden platter. *But not so clever that they didn't manage to get lost in the darkness.* If she hadn't guided them out, they'd be there still.

At the time, she'd wanted to keep them from perishing there in the bowels of the earth. She thought that perhaps they'd find their way to Vivienne, who might have gotten free and regained possession of Excalibur.

If this was true, she needed to know about it.

The poison she had given to Mordred—a concoction made from the toxin of a puffer fish and the venom of a rattlesnake, both attained from sorcerers from distant lands at a very high price—could never be reproduced. It was the only thing that could have bested the power of Excalibur.

One of the two serving women picked up the platter to take into the dining hall, and Morgan followed her to the doorway but hung back on the kitchen side as the serving woman went into the dining hall.

Standing just out of sight, she observed the sisters taking their seats at the long dining table. As she stood there, she noticed that they were wearing shawls. It wasn't especially chilly—so what were they up to?

"Why are you lurking about in the doorway, Millicent?" Helen scolded as she bustled by with the braised rabbit that would be the main course that night. "Go check that the mince pie isn't burning."

Morgan shot her an annoyed glance and maintained her position at the side of the doorway. The one called Rowena, the only one of them that was more than pretty, that was actually beautiful, sat slumped at the table. Lovesick, no doubt. Fool!

Morgan grinned. What a stroke of luck it had been to have the very thing she sought come walking right into the forest.

Excalibur!

If she possessed Excalibur, she would not have to care what Vivienne and her twelve offspring did. And now it was so close!

She would have believed that the handsome fellow who bore it on his hip really was a beggar—that he had stolen the sword—if she had not recognized that crippled, useless hand. The moment she had spied that, she'd known him at once. In the Welsh dialect of his hometown his name had been Bedwyr Bedrydant. It meant "Bedivere of the Perfect Sinews," and it suited him well. It was hard to say what part of him was more delicious, that gorgeous face, with its high cheekbones and piercing eyes, or the fabulous form.

It was a shame about the hand, but obviously what they said about him was true—being one-handed had not impaired his fighting skill. She saw that for herself today when she'd assumed the shape of a fighting boulder, a rock soldier, in order to knock Excalibur out of his hands. With a wince, she gazed down at her bruised and sliced arms, which still bore the injuries he'd dealt her when he'd hacked at her with Excalibur. She hadn't realized what a formidable opponent he would be. With Excalibur in his hand, he was nearly unbeatable.

She'd changed back into mouse form once he'd won the battle and had run halfway to the manor when she looked back to see him with Rowena. And, oh, how they had gazed at one another. Morgan had seen the face of love before and these two had an extreme case.

Bedivere might be an able knight, but now she knew his weakness, Sir Ethan's lovely daughter.

She continued observing the girls all through the meal. Occasionally she pretended to busy herself with a task, but mostly she watched their every move.

Sir Ethan was out of sorts, grumbling surly replies to their comments. The sisters, though, seemed strangely unconcerned that they were to be bolted into their room. In fact, they appeared to be nearly giddy—with the exception of Rowena.

After dessert, Sir Ethan left his daughters under Mary's supervision. That's when Morgan saw what was happening. Eleanore had hidden one of the small oil lamps under her shawl and the one they called Cecily had taken another one.

Where would they need light but in the tunnels of darkness!

If they were going into the tunnels again, she was too. In a moment, she was once again in her mouse form.

"Millicent!" Helen shouted in an exasperated voice. "Where have you gone off to now?"

Morgan heard Helen's voice like a banging gong and snickered in satisfaction as she darted through the dining hall, keeping close to the baseboards. Fast as she was, they left her behind with their much longer strides. When she arrived at their bedchamber, the door was shut. Mouse instinct kicked in and she realized she could squeeze through the tightest of spaces. In a second she was inside the bedchamber.

The room was a whirl of activity as they threw off their shawls and pulled off their dresses, tossing them to the floor. The sisters donned the nightgowns, and the delicate slippers were tucked under each bed.

The stolen lamps were shoved together and covered with a blanket in the corner before the sisters hopped into their beds, pulling the covers high.

Morgan, her whiskers twitching with anticipation, hid behind a chest and watched. Mary entered and behind her were maids carrying chamber pots. "Do you young ladies have everything you require?" she asked as the maids left.

Brianna yawned and stretched. "Everything, thank you, Mary."

"Good night, Mary," the other sisters sang out, almost in one voice.

"Good night, girls. Sleep well," Mary bade them. She left and the sound of the heavy bolt being slid shut echoed in the quiet room.

First one of the small oil lamps was lit, then the other. Then Morgan heard the scratching of the heavy bed against the floor as they pushed it away from the trapdoor.

They spoke eagerly, but their voices were too loud, their tones too distorted by the intense volume for her to decipher what they were saying even though they whispered.

They put on their slippers and then pulled up the trapdoors. Drum beats and whistles floated up out of the opening. The young women began beating their feet to the lively tune, swaying and twirling to the vibrant music.

One at a time, they descended into the hole in the floor. Morgan seized her moment and scampered down into the dark space along with them.

In her mouse form, Morgan was blasted by the music in the passageways, just as she had been the night before. That was why, when the sisters found her, she had been in such a hurry to get out of the tunnel. Now her ears ached again and, letting the sisters get ahead of her, she transformed into her own form—neither Millicent, the hag of a servant, nor a mouse, but Morgan le Fey, the sorceress.

That was better. Pressing her palms to her aching ears to soothe them, she hung back behind the sisters. Since they now carried lamps, it wasn't difficult to keep them in sight as they wound their way through the passages.

She followed them until they came out to the high cavern of softly glowing stalactites and stalagmites. There, the sisters went to the edge of the large underground lake. Morgan hung back in the shadows of a tunnel as the one named Ione took off her slippers and stuck her foot in the shimmering water. "It's not cold at all," she told her sisters. She impulsively pulled her nightgown over her head and plunged, naked, into the water.

Tossing off their slippers and nightgowns the other sisters followed her example and were soon all swimming in the glittering lake. Only Rowena stayed behind, draped on a rock, deep in thought.

Morgan drew in a sharp breath of realization. She knew where they were, what this place was! Why hadn't she recognized it immediately?

This was the place where Vivienne's lake had settled to, deep in the earth's depths, when she, Morgan, had cursed it to be hidden below ground forever. These foolish girls were swimming right over their mother's head as she languished below them, trapped in a magical bubble!

"It's not as deep as I would have thought," said the sister called Mathilde. "I can touch the bottom."

Ione and Chloe both dove under. Morgan wondered if Vivienne was able to see them from below. Was it possible for them to see her?

Morgan didn't really know, for certain, and she shifted uneasily from foot to foot, suddenly worried that these young women were so close to their mother.

At least Rowena had stayed out, probably mooning over her Bedivere. Of them all, she seemed to be the one who had inherited her mother's talent for second sight. She'd be the one most sensitive to Vivienne's presence.

Thinking of their mother reminded Morgan of how resourceful and gifted Vivienne had been in the days before her entrapment. If she knew her daughters were right above her—and she might—who knew what trick she'd employ to attract their attention and enlist their aid?

Morgan decided it would be in her best interest to throw these sisters off the trail. And she'd watched them long enough to know just what they longed for—adventure, parties, romance.

She had just the spell that would make it happen.

From her shadowed hiding place, Morgan began murmuring the incantations that would conjure the magic she desired. She mumbled on as she watched the sisters climbing out of the dark lake, their bodies dazzling with glimmers of phosphorescence that clung to their glistening, wet skin.

Sparks leapt between Morgan's fingernails as she worked the first of her charms.

"My nightgown!" Ashlynn cried in surprise, lifting the garment. "It's a gorgeous gown!"

"Mine is also," Helewise told them as she picked up a turquoise satin dress festooned with pearls at the bosom.

All of the nightgowns were now transformed into incredible gowns made of brocades, silks, and satins. They were decorated with pearls, jewels, ribbons, bows, and lace; each gown exactly suited the coloring, body, and personality of each young woman.

Amazed, they quickly put them on. As they dressed, their hair began to move on its own, twisting into elaborate, elegant coiffures of ringlets, braids, buns, and loose curls, some strung with diamonds or pearls, others adorned with shining golden pins and gem-studded barrettes.

Rowena's nightgown changed itself right on her

body into a deep blue satin with draping sleeves and a daring neckline. Her hair was now caught in a swirl of braids at her nape, bundled with a net of sapphire stones.

As the sisters admired one another, more sparks flew between Morgan's fingernails, and six golden barges appeared on the sparkling lake, all of them silently moving toward the shore where the sisters stood in their gowns.

As the barges grew nearer, the sisters saw the creatures standing on board. Each barge carried two figures. They were dressed richly in elegant robes with the vests, leggings, and boots of dashing young men. But from the neck up they were stags. Each had the head and many-pointed antlers of a large male deer.

Morgan reserved the last part of her enchantment for the sisters. With a final jolt of energy between her fingers, she lifted any reservations or misgivings they might feel about embarking on a journey with these strange, virile creatures. Even Rowena, completely smitten as she was with her love for Bedivere, could not resist the lure of a possible adventure. Morgan had clouded their minds so that they saw these stag princes as completely acceptable escorts.

The stag princes moored their barges and leapt over the sides, heedless of the water splashing around their boots. With gallant bows, each approached one of the sisters and offered a hand.

The sisters took the hands that were offered and

let themselves be lifted onto the barges, two to a vessel. Then the barges smoothly floated off.

Morgan slumped against the wall of the passage, exhausted by the effort of conjuring such an elaborate spell. The stag princes would take the sisters to an enchanted island at the far end of the lake where they would feast and dance with them until dawn. Any time the sisters appeared here in the cavern, the stags would come to meet them.

"Vivienne's brats eliminated," Vivienne said, satisfied with and, she felt, justifiably proud of her resourceful solution.

PART THREE

The Enchanted Ones

CHAPTER SEVENTEEN
Vivienne's Despair

Vivienne wept with rage and frustration. She had seen her children. They were right above her! She had pounded on the impenetrable barrier and screamed to attract their attention. All the while they swam, blithely unaware of her desperate cries.

They had grown up to be so lovely, like mermaids with their long hair floating around them. But she had only counted eleven of them. Where was her Rowena, her daughter with the second sight? Vivienne had known that even as a baby the girl had the sight.

It was Rowena who could see into the scrying bowl. Rowena was the one she might be able to contact.

But then there were barges, and she had sensed magic. Her daughters had floated away from her. Where had they gone? What had happened?

Hours later they had returned on the golden barges. She'd seen odd deer men reflected in the lake. They were familiar to her. She had seen similar creatures during her training on Avalon. They were figures of romance, attentive and radiating male energy.

But they were creatures of magic, illusions meant to captivate a female's heart, with no true substance.

They bore every indication of having been called up by Morgan le Fey.

This was very bad. Why was Morgan near her girls? Where was their father? Why wasn't he protecting them?

Consumed with desperate rage, she hurled herself against the surface of the lake and was thrown back down to the bottom by its impenetrable field of resistance.

CHAPTER EIGHTEEN
Bedivere in Love

Bedivere had returned to Glastonbury and washed with water from the town well. He'd even used the edge of his own sword to shave the rough bristles from his face.

But the next day, when he returned to the forest for their arranged meeting, Rowena did not come. After waiting by the boulder for two hours, he walked to the wall and found the break through which she must have come.

He felt hurt, angry, and humiliated. She'd played him for a fool, toyed with him! He glanced at his crippled hand and was filled with shame and insecurity. When she'd noticed it, she must have been repulsed, although she'd been too polite to show it. Now, though, she wanted no part of him.

A movement on the other side of the wall made him turn his attention toward the sound. Crouching, he saw a boy's legs in boots. A mat was pushed against the opening, and the boy settled onto it.

"Boy!" Bedivere summoned him in a whisper.

The startled goose boy put his freckled face to the opening. "Who goes there?"

"Has something happened to Rowena who lives within?" he asked.

"Locked up," the goose boy revealed with a youthful lack of suspicion. "Her father, Sir Ethan, discovered she was going into the forest through this very opening. Now he has locked in all his daughters and will soon repair this wall."

"Thanks for your information," Bedivere said as he got to his feet.

He was elated to hear this news. She hadn't been *able* to come to him. It wasn't that she'd *chosen* not to meet him.

He had saved young women who were trapped in towers, had even helped one get past an ogre. He'd rescued all the women of a town from giants! Freeing the woman who had captured his heart from an overprotective father shouldn't prove too daunting.

He went to the front gate and rapped on it. When no one came to answer, he ran the hilt of his sword, the one he had tucked into his belt, along the wrought iron. "Hello?" he shouted. "Hello?"

After several minutes of this, the grand front door opened and a plump, elderly woman came out to see who was making the noise. "I am Sir Bedivere, knight of the Round Table." He introduced himself with a gallant bow. "I seek a word with Sir Ethan."

The woman scrutinized him skeptically. "I will

bring you a meal from the kitchen," she said. "Wait there."

Bedivere realized how he must look to her. "I am no beggar," he called to her, but she was already halfway back to the door.

"I'll send someone out with food," she called over her shoulder just before disappearing inside.

Bedivere was stumped. He no longer had his horse, or his companions, or his armor to make him appear formidable. Even if he'd had these things, who would he attack? Certainly not this kindly house servant who was willing to feed one she believed to be a raving lunatic wandering in the forest.

And if he gained an audience with Sir Ethan, why should Sir Ethan allow him to see Rowena? Even with a shaved face he remained a disheveled figure.

Bedivere walked back along the wall and gazed up at the high windows. His heart leapt as he saw a slim figure with long, coppery hair appear at one of the windows. He raised his hand to attract her attention, but in the next second, she was gone.

CHAPTER NINETEEN
Sir Ethan's Next Plan

Sir Ethan stared at the slippers lined up in a row outside the bedchamber that his daughters shared. He could not believe what he saw. They were torn, dirty, utterly destroyed.

Again!

This was the third morning in a row that the slippers had turned up in this condition.

He had done everything he could think of. He'd changed all the locks. The goose boy had guarded the opening in the wall until he'd been able to bring in a mason to repair it. Mary was now with them every minute of the day. *It will take a greater mind than mine to unravel this mystery!* he thought in despair as he stomped away from the line of tattered slippers.

And then he stopped short, struck with an inspiration.

That was it! He needed to recruit some help, a greater mind—but from where?

He sat on a carved hallway bench to think about this further. Many clever young men—students, merchants, and soldiers—lived within Glastonbury. Each might lend a unique perspective to solving the problem. What if he offered a prize to the man who could tell him where the girls were going at night and how they were getting there?

He recalled his conversation with Rowena. His daughters were of an age where they required husbands. For years he had meant to begin the process of finding suitable candidates.

He had never done it, though.

There always seemed to be more pressing, more immediate concerns to attend to. And there was an element of avoidance; he knew it was true. He didn't *want* to entrust one of his precious daughters to some unreliable young man. The fellow might appear to be solid at first, but it took a great test to tell what he was really made of. Ethan's years of military service had taught him that.

Still, it had to be done, this business of finding husbands for them, and now might be an excellent time to begin. A young man clever enough to figure out this puzzle would certainly seem bright enough to make a good life for one of his daughters.

Of course! He would allow the young man who won to select one of his daughters to marry!

Brilliant!

He frowned and folded his arms, thinking. How would he go about doing this? A sign would have to be made. The monks were skilled calligraphers, always transcribing copies of books; he'd make a donation and get one of them to write the announcement. Then he'd go into Glastonbury and post it for all to see.

He stood, full of new purpose, but a sudden concern made him pause. What if some undesirable fellow won the contest—a person of low moral character or of meager social position, or both?

He shook off the thought. This was too excellent an idea to forsake because of idle worries that would probably never come to pass. The majority of people were, after all, usually fairly decent. And this man would be brilliant.

Putting aside his concerns, Sir Ethan went off to saddle his horses for the ride to the monastery. When he got there, he was greeted by Brother Joseph.

At first, Sir Ethan did not recognize the monk who had tended to him so many years ago when he had gone out searching for Vivienne, but after they had spoken for a few moments he recalled the voice and gestures.

Brother Joseph seemed aware of the look of recognition from Sir Ethan, and he returned it. "What news of your wife?" he asked.

Sir Ethan shook his head. "I often wonder if she was indeed a forest spirit as you told me those many years ago," he confided.

"It is surely possible," Brother Joseph said as they walked together through the quiet monastery halls. "The mystic Island of Avalon is said to be very near to here, though few know the way to it. The wizards, priestesses, sorcerers, and sorceresses of old come from there. It is the repository of powerful magic, and it often spills over into our world."

Sir Ethan recalled the otherworldly beauty of his wife, and it filled him with nostalgia for the old days when they were together. He remembered the terrifying fear he'd known when this monk had suggested that their children might be figments of enchanted imagination rather than real little girls.

"My daughters have proved real enough," he told Brother Joseph. "They remind me daily of their mother. As such, they are both a comfort and a torment to me."

"Do you see any signs that they have abilities from the other realms?" Brother Joseph asked as they reached a room where monks stood at separate podiums quietly copying Latin words from thick books.

"No," Sir Ethan said. Although he had noticed a faraway look in the eyes of his youngest, Rowena, a look that reminded him powerfully of her mother, he thought it more prudent not to mention it.

After he'd made a considerable donation to the monastery, a monk named Brother Theodosius began work on the announcement Sir Ethan wanted made. The monk wasn't the monastery's finest calligrapher. His work was, in fact, a bit sloppy, but for sign making it would do.

Soon Sir Ethan possessed a good-size parchment with the words he desired in an elegant, artistic script. They read:

Sir Ethan of Colchester announces a contest open to all men from the ages of eighteen to thirty.

*He who is able to unravel the riddle
and solve the problem posed to him
will win
the hand of one of Sir Ethan's twelve beautiful daughters
in marriage.
The winner may choose his own bride, who
comes with a handsome dowry.*

Brother Theodosius handed the rolled parchment to him. "Ride with care for these are perilous times," the monk said to him. "Have you heard the news that our King Arthur was slain in battle?"

Sir Ethan stepped back, aghast at these words. He had great respect for Arthur, the son of Uther Pendragon, the chieftain in whose army he had once served. He owed his title to the older man, and he'd heard that Pendragon's heir was a noble king. He had assuredly brought stability to the country by uniting the lesser kingdoms and warding off outside invaders. "By whom is he slain?" he asked.

"Mordred, his own kinsman. The knights of the Round Table were all slain along with him, every last one."

Sir Ethan shook his head woefully. "Such brave and noble men! We'll not see the like of them ever again."

With this troubling news on his mind, Sir Ethan rode into Glastonbury and posted his new sign on a thick tree in the town square.

He watched as eligible young men gathered around

the sign and began to nod and murmur excitedly to one another. Inside of a half hour the murmuring grew into boasting and posturing as the men tried to scare off potential rivals.

Sir Ethan felt satisfied that this plan would work perfectly. Any one of the young men gathered around his announcement struck him as a suitable enough husband for one of his daughters. They might not be as noble as a knight of the Round Table—but that was no longer even a remote possibility, it seemed. That noble breed had disappeared, gone like the fierce and brave unicorns of old.

These lesser men, who appeared to be merchants, like him, and also tradesmen, itinerant soldiers, and scholars, crowded around the sign. Occasionally a man came by who seemed to be of high-born stock, possibly a duke or count. Sir Ethan was pleased to see even these wealthy gentlemen stop to read his sign.

His eyes narrowed with concern, however, when he caught sight of a scruffy beggar quietly reading the announcement. He didn't like the fiery determination burning in the bedraggled pauper's dark eyes.

CHAPTER TWENTY
Eleanore Revolts

Eleanore's hands went to her hips as she scowled darkly at her father. Her sisters, who surrounded her there in their bedchamber, all wore similar expressions. "How could you?" she cried, made bold by her genuine outrage. "You've offered one of us as a prize? A *prize!*"

"Rowena told me you wanted husbands," Sir Ethan defended himself.

The sisters turned their angry looks on Rowena.

"I said we wanted to meet young men and fall in love," she insisted. "I didn't say I wanted to be given away like a prize *pig*. This is a different thing entirely."

"What if some arrogant idiot wants me for his wife?" Ione fretted. "He'll always be telling me what to do, and it will always be the wrong thing that shouldn't be done at all . . . because he's an idiot."

"If he's an idiot he won't win," Sir Ethan pointed out.

"*Win!*" Eleanore cried. "He'll *win* one of us—a flesh and blood human being, one of your own daughters— as a *prize!* Can't you see how *wrong* this is?"

"Eleanore, I recognize that you girls have been

sheltered," Sir Ethan began angrily, "so I understand that you are perhaps unaware of the ways of the world, but you might be interested to learn that young women frequently, in fact nearly *always*, are given in marriages arranged by their parents."

"Well, that's insane!" Rowena burst out, throwing her arms out at her sides.

Sir Ethan frowned at her insolence.

"She's right," Eleanore backed up Rowena.

"*This* argument is insane," Sir Ethan exploded, clearly out of patience. "We can end this contest right now. All you need to do is tell me why your slippers are ruined every single morning even though when you enter your bedchamber they are in perfect condition! Where do you go? How do you get out?"

The sisters glanced at one another from the corners of their eyes. Eleanore knew what they were thinking because she was thinking the same thing.

Nothing could compel them to give up the dancing they'd enjoyed these past three nights. Of course they knew that their stag escorts weren't potential husbands, but how could they resist them? They were so charmingly attentive, fetching the girls food and drink, dancing with them until dawn.

The island the golden barges carried them to was a paradise. Icy fountains of bubbling drinks flowed without stop. Musicians strolled constantly, playing every kind of lively, exciting music.

Ornate mahogany tables groaned under the

weight of delicious foods, some that they had never even seen before like the tart star-shaped fruit and the tiny, glistening black fish eggs served on toast that they so especially loved.

And most of all, they danced, danced like they were on fire. The musicians never tired of playing, and the sisters were on their slippered feet nearly the entire time, stopping only to refresh themselves with food and drink.

The stag princes partnered them, moving with animal vigor, leaping, spinning, carrying the sisters over their heads as they jumped high into the air. Their large deep eyes caressed attentively and it didn't matter that they were not directly amorous. The way they danced—holding the sisters tight one moment, throwing them wildly the next—conveyed an exciting sensuality that was thrilling in itself.

In part, they were aware that this was a fantasy, maybe even an enchantment of some kind, but they felt powerless to resist it. It was every hope of exotic excitement suddenly become reality, and they were completely enthralled by it. On the luxuriant, thrilling island in the middle of the glittering, fathomless underground lake, they felt beautiful, desirable, utterly seduced.

How could they give that up?

No. They couldn't—not for anything.

"If you will not answer me then you will abide by the terms of my contest!" Sir Ethan bellowed, reddening with rage. "I will have the servants remove the door on the room adjacent to this one. We will set up a sleeping quarter for the young man, and he will know your every move."

"That's indecent!" Gwendolyn objected. "How will we dress?"

Sir Ethan reddened slightly with embarrassment. "We'll install a drape over the doorway, and I will threaten any young man with death who behaves improperly toward you."

"I don't want some hairy old man sleeping nearby, practically in the bedchamber with us," Isolde grumbled.

"Enough!" Sir Ethan shouted. "You will be discovered eventually, and one of you will wed whoever uncovers your secret." He banged the door shut behind him as he stormed out of the room.

As always, the sisters looked toward Eleanore to tell them what to do. This time, though, she wasn't sure how to advise them. "I think . . . ," she began slowly, settling on a bed, "that what we must do is be very, very sure that we are not discovered. To be found out would mean a terrible fate for one of us and the end of happiness for all of us."

"But what if the young man who wins is wonderful?" Bronwyn asked.

"What if he's not?" Eleanore countered. "Wouldn't you rather choose for yourself?"

"Absolutely!" Rowena agreed passionately.

Eleanore studied her intently. Rowena had met

someone when she was beyond the manor wall, she was more sure of it than ever. Even on the island, though she danced and feasted, she was more reserved than the others.

"When will we ever get the chance to choose a husband for ourselves?" Cecily said. "That day might never come. Isn't it better that one of us has a chance to get free of this imprisonment? Maybe that sister could help the others?"

Eleanore sighed in frustration. "It's all possible, I suppose, but which of you wants to stop going to the island?"

After a moment's silence, Rowena spoke quietly. "I do." They looked at her incredulously, but she continued. "Didn't we set out to find our mother? Have we completely given up on that plan?"

"Have you seen something in your scrying bowl?" Eleanore inquired warily. She loved the island and didn't wish to be diverted from its pleasures, but she felt obligated to ask.

Rowena nodded. "I see a sad woman. Sometimes she weeps; at other times she stares blankly, as if defeated. At times she pounds on the walls and screams."

"Are you sure you haven't imagined this?" Eleanore asked.

"No. I'm not sure," Rowena admitted. "This entire business of seeing things beyond the reach of normal sight confounds and confuses me. In a way, I wish I wasn't seeing these disturbing things, but I am."

"Perhaps you just *wish* to see the things that you do," Isolde suggested.

"I wish *not* to see them," Rowena said, disagreeing with a disparaging laugh.

"We have no real proof that our mother is calling to us," said Eleanore in a voice of one in charge. "The evidence is that she is not even alive. What we know is that we have been incarcerated in this prison of a home without the normal social opportunities to which any young woman is entitled."

"What opportunities?" Brianna asked eagerly.

Eleanore sat forward as she warmed to her topic. "I have read the books that the servants bring in, particularly the romances that are penned in France. Young women our age should be going to balls, parties, and lavish dinners. Handsome young men should be begging for our hands in marriage and languishing for want of a kiss. The eldest of us might already be mothers with homes of our own. But the insane behavior of our parents—a mother who abandoned us, a father who is maniacally overprotective—has denied us all that we deserve."

"I never saw it that way before," said Helewise thoughtfully.

"Well, that's how it seems to me," Eleanore insisted. "And now some strange twist of fate has given to us what we have lacked. Our father wishes to thwart even that, and so we must outwit him at his own game."

"How will we accomplish that?" Ione inquired.

"I have a thought," Eleanore continued. "There is much magic surrounding us in our nightly revels. I will ask my stag for some kind of sleeping draught that will render our nightly guardian too sleepy to follow us. Although my stag never speaks, he seems to understand me when I request a drink or some food of him. Perhaps, then, he can aid me with this request, as well."

"What if he doesn't know of any such sleeping potion?" Mathilde considered.

Eleanore pressed her lips together as she thought. "I don't know," she confessed. "I'm simply going to hope that he does."

Glancing out the window, she saw that it was nearly dark. "Come, let's move the bed," she instructed her sisters. "It's time to go."

CHAPTER TWENTY-ONE
Bedivere Is Tempted

Bedivere coughed harshly into the sleeve of his tunic, and his chest ached with the effort. The nights spent on the dirty mat in the disease-infested alley of beggars had caused him to come down with congestion in his head and chest. He felt his forehead and determined that it was warmer than normal.

He could not let it stop him, though. Pausing at the town well, he drew up a bucket of water and poured it over his head, drenching his hair and clothing. It was not a proper bath, like the kind he'd enjoyed in a marble tub back in Camelot, but it was better than nothing and it was all he really felt capable of at the moment.

He needed to get back to the manor, and he had to do it before someone else beat him to the challenge. This contest posted by Sir Ethan was his chance to get inside the manor to see Rowena. He clung to the belief that she'd have him if he won the competition, and this was a prize beyond any measure.

As he walked down the road, he saw other men who seemed to be headed in the same direction. Some rode fine horses and were dressed richly.

Others affected a scholarly air, and still others were attended by retinues of servants who carried them aloft on fancy pallets. Bedivere tried to keep in mind that he was Sir Bedivere of the Round Table and not let himself become demoralized by his present state, but the fits of coughing that overtook him and the sweaty fatigue his illness induced did nothing to help his frame of mind.

He attempted to arrive at the manor before the others by cutting into the forest in hopes of finding a shortcut. He was an excellent navigator and was encouraged that he was making good time until he came over the hill just before the manor.

The forest was infested with men setting up camp outside the manor's front gate. As he came closer, he saw Sir Ethan appear at the front gate and step out in front of it. There was immediately a rush of men who crowded around him. Bedivere hurried forward and made his way to the front.

"Thank you all for coming," Sir Ethan spoke to them. He nodded at the gilded box he held. "I have here numbers inscribed on cards. I will hand them out and they will tell you the order in which you are to be allowed inside to test your wits in this competition."

He opened the lid and took out his numbered cards. Bedivere stepped forward along with the others. A fight broke out between two men directly in front of him as one pushed ahead of the other. Bedivere seized the opportunity to work his way around them and get to the head of the crowd.

When he finally stood in front of Sir Ethan, the man eyed him with disapproval. To Bedivere's dismay, at that moment a fit of coughing overtook him, doubling him over.

"I am sorry for your illness my good man," Sir Ethan told him when he had recovered and stood awaiting his card, "but I cannot risk having my household infected with whatever ails you. With the plague and pox so rampant in parts of our countryside, I simply cannot allow you to enter my home in your condition."

"I assure you this is but a temporary ailment and will soon be done with," Bedivere tried to persuade him.

Sir Ethan studied him as if struck by the way in which his knightly manner seemed at odds with his beggar's appearance. Then another man shoved in front of him and Sir Ethan turned his attention to that man. Bedivere found himself jostled rudely to the back of the crowd.

Sweat was now gleaming on his forehead and he found it difficult to stand. Leaning against a tree, he gazed up at the window where he had thought he might have seen Rowena standing.

There, again, with the sunlight glinting off the window, he saw a figure with long coppery hair. This time, she raised her hand and pressed it against the glass. She saw him. He was sure of it.

He envisioned her face, those green changeable

eyes, and the sensuous curve of her lips. Pressing his cheek against the tree's bark for its coolness, he felt his spirit lift from his body and he was, once again, on the boulder in the forest. And she was there, too.

This time they needed no words. He held her tightly, with his good hand firmly on the small of her back, as they kissed. He was no longer sick, as she wrapped her arms around his neck, pulling him closer to her. He felt the firm softness of her body pressed against his, and he burned to have her next to him, knowing that they were meant for one another in every way possible.

Another lifting of the spirit—and he abruptly opened his eyes. A darting glance to the window told him she was no longer there.

He found himself staring into the face of a man dressed richly in a cape of fur-trimmed red and gold brocade. Beneath it he wore a thick gold vest and black leggings. His boots gleamed with polish. "I will pay you a king's ransom for that sword," he said, nodding toward Excalibur at Bedivere's hip.

Bedivere shook his head heavily, realizing that the fever and congestion were with him again. "This sword is not for sale," he replied.

"Look at your condition," the man pointed out. "I saw that Sir Ethan turned you away at the gate." He produced a velvet pouch from beneath his elegant cloak. "Think what this could do for you," he said, opening the pouch to reveal the sparkle of gold and precious gems. "With this you would not have to win one of his daughters. You would have no need of her dowry. You could walk in and purchase the one of your choosing. And I suspect you have already selected the one you desire."

Bedivere straightened warily and, with a warrior's instincts for danger, his hand went for Excalibur's hilt, preparing to pull it from its scabbard. Who was this man? "How do you know these things?" he challenged.

The man smiled slightly and continued without answering the question. "What good is a dead man's sword to you who wants no more of fighting and knightly battles? Why cling to it when it could buy you what your heart truly desires?"

The man pulled one of Sir Ethan's cards from the pocket of his cloak. It had the number one inked on it. "I will add this to the price," he continued. "It will get you into the manor and the fortune I pay you will do the rest."

Despite his suspicions about this man, Bedivere couldn't stop himself from envisioning what a fortune could do for him. He could have a manor of his own, one worthy of Rowena. They could live there without care. Sir Ethan would never turn him away if he arrived arrayed in kingly fashion.

The man was correct that Excalibur could help him attain what he most desired, Rowena. He might never find this Lady of the Lake, might spend the rest of his life searching for her to no avail. Why not sell Excalibur and get what he wanted?

He began to unbuckle his belt, which held the sheathed sword.

The man held the pouch and the card out to him.

Bedivere took off the sword and scabbard, but then stopped. He remembered the trusting expression on Arthur's face when he had commissioned him to return Excalibur to the Lady of the Lake.

How could he betray his promise to Arthur?

He'd promised his king. He'd promised his dearest friend.

He was—still and always, though no one else knew it—Sir Bedivere, the last knight of the Round Table, whose code of honor insisted that a promise was a sacred trust.

He fastened Excalibur back onto his belt. "Thank you for your offer, but I cannot accept it," he said with some remaining reluctance. It hurt to decline, no matter how honor-bound he felt.

The man put the pouch and card back into his cloak and angrily drew a sword. "I have been reasonable," he snarled softly with silky menace. "If you will not sell me the sword I will fight you for it."

Summoning what strength he could call upon, Bedivere gripped Excalibur and drew. Blade clashed against blade as the two men fought fiercely. The man slashed a tear in Bedivere's tunic. Bedivere returned the blow with a piercing thrust to the man's side.

The moment Excalibur touched him, the man burst into a flame that was sucked downward into the Earth.

Astonished, Bedivere leapt backward, clutching Excalibur. He recalled his fight with the rock soldier. At the time he had thought he had simply run across some malevolent forest spirit. But now he realized that some powerful sorcerer or sorceress was aware that he carried the dead king's sword and was determined to take it from him.

He now understood why Arthur had been so adamant that he return the sword to his kinswoman. Its magic must be more powerful than he had even realized if dark forces would go to such lengths to attain it. He would need to be vigilant at every moment until it was safely delivered.

The effort of the battle he'd just fought combined with his sickness suddenly overtook him. Leaning heavily against a tree for support, he slid down its side until he was sitting on the ground, drenched in feverish sweat.

A man on horseback stopped in front of him. "You appear unwell," he observed. "Can I offer you transport back to town?"

He glanced back to the window where he had seen Rowena. He couldn't yet stand to be parted from her nearness. "I thank you, but no," he declined, appreciative of the kind gesture. "Why are you leaving?"

"Although these others are all camping out, I have no time to wait around for my chance," he explained as he took one of Sir Ethan's cards from his vest. He dropped it down onto Bedivere's lap. "Have it if you like. It's sure to move you up the line." Without a further comment, he rode off through the woods.

Bedivere turned the card over in his hand. The number two was inscribed upon it.

What luck! He had a chance now, but would the challenge thwart the man who went before him? What if the first man won his Rowena away from him? Bedivere was sure she would be the sister who was chosen. What man could resist her?

What would he do then—fight the man for her? How could he justify battling another honorable man to steal his fairly won prize? How could he bear not to?

He could only fervently, deeply hope that the rival who would go before him would fail.

PART FOUR

The Contest

Chapter Twenty-two
Eleanore Wields Her Potion

The next night Eleanore sat on her bed and watched as the first man in Sir Ethan's competition entered the bedchamber with a slight swagger, clomping in with heavy boots. An involuntary rush of excitement surged through her. He wasn't bad looking, with thick blond hair and broad shoulders.

She found herself sitting up a bit straighter, the better to display her womanly assets, only to notice that several other of her sisters, each of whom sat on her own bed, were doing the same.

"Hello, ladies," he greeted them pleasantly, grinning and glancing from one to the other, no doubt selecting his prize. "I hear you've been naughty girls."

"Wouldn't you like to know," Eleanore teased flirtatiously.

He grinned even more widely than before, and his hungry expression made a hot blush rise in Eleanore's cheeks. "Indeed, I *would* like to know. Your father has told me to keep a sharp eye on you and find out where you've been going."

Right then Mary scurried in followed by two serving women, one carrying a basin and pitcher, the other holding a stack of towels. "Right this way, Lord Liddington," she said authoritatively as she led him into the small room adjacent to the bedchamber. "We have made up a bed for you, and the maids have brought your washing needs."

Mary noticed the lingering glances Lord Liddington was sending Eleanore's way and frowned. "I'm sure you recall Sir Ethan's warning regarding any improper advances toward his daughters," she reminded him firmly.

"I most surely do," he assured her, rolling his eyes at Eleanore before Mary pulled the heavy drape and hid him from view.

She stood in front of the draped doorway with her arms folded like a protective lioness. "Get dressed for bed, girls," she ordered crossly.

Mary had made it known that she did not like this whole idea. Men did not belong in a bedchamber with young women, not even next door. She'd had her bed carried into the room in order to act as chaperone. But that only seemed to put her further out of sorts. Eleanore guessed that she already missed the privacy of her own bedchamber.

When the girls were dressed in their nightgowns and were settled under their covers, Mary pulled aside the drape that separated Lord Liddington's sleeping area.

Eleanore peeked over her pillow and could see him straddling the chair next to his bed. He caught her eye and smiled. She returned his smile but pulled it into a frown when Mary glowered at her warningly.

"Rowena, come away from that window and get into bed," Mary barked.

Eleanore didn't like the way Lord Liddington followed Rowena's every move as she crossed the room to get into bed. With the moonlight behind her, a person could see her whole form through that nightgown. Couldn't she have worn a thicker one?

"Now I will be lying on my bed with my eyes closed, but I won't really be asleep," Mary told them all. "My advice to you girls is to stay put and present your slippers in perfect condition in the morning. In that way you'll bring things back to normal and make this whole troublesome business of strange men in your bedchamber go away."

A mouse scampered along the baseboards and Mary hurled the pillow from her bed at it. "Get out of here, you pest." The mouse disappeared into a hole and Mary picked up the pillow. "I don't know if we're overrun with mice or if the same one keeps pestering us. It's not as though you can easily identify one from the other."

"That one looked like it had a cut in its side," Eleanore observed. "Maybe it had a battle with a cat. From now on you'll be able to tell if it's the same one."

"Yes ... well ... sleep now, girls," Mary said as she lay back on her bed fully clothed.

The light stayed on in Lord Liddington's area.

Eleanore peeked above her pillow and smiled at him again. She counted the minutes until Mary began to snore. The sisters knew Mary was a sound sleeper. Through the years they'd gone to her room to rouse her when one or another of them was sick in the night, and they had found it impossible to wake the snoring woman. They were counting on her deep slumber this night.

Once her thunderous snores became regular, Eleanore reached under her bed and found the jug of cider Ione had taken from the kitchen earlier. Into it, Eleanore had poured the contents of a silken packet containing a mix of some powder with finely chopped herbs.

The night before Eleanore had asked her stag escort for a concoction to induce deep, deep sleep, and he had gone away and returned with this packet. He had shown her how to mix it in a liquid-filled cup until it was totally dissolved.

Reaching under the bed again, she pulled out two goblets. She threw off her blanket and slid out of bed. With one deep breath to steady her nerves, she sauntered over to Lord Liddington and pulled the drape over the door closed behind her. "Hello, Lord Liddington," she said.

"Call me Edgar," he replied. He sat back in his chair and appraised her merrily. "What have you got there?"

"I thought we might share something to drink,

Edgar," she said, setting the goblets down on the nightstand beside the basin and pitcher.

"No wine for me," he replied. "I must stay sharp and see what you bad women are up to."

"It's only cider," she said, offering him the open jug to smell.

He took hold of her outstretched arm and drew her toward him. Wrapping his other hand around her waist, he pulled her down so that she was sitting on his broad leg, his eyes twinkling at her.

Eleanore couldn't help but respond to him. She caught a scent of pine on his clothing and it stirred something within her. She found that she was inclined to lean up against him seductively, a move he gladly allowed.

He began planting small kisses along her neck as he stroked her collarbone. "Tell me, my lady, where have you and your sisters been going at night?" he murmured seductively to her. "Tell me so that I might marry you and we can do more of this in the privacy of our own home."

Eleanore was enjoying his touch and his offer tempted her. She saw herself with him, alone, embracing and kissing, their bodies pressed against one another for endless moments without interruption.

Then she thought of what she would be losing: her nightly dances on the underground island with its mystery and luxury. She pulled away from him slightly. "Let's have some cider," she suggested. "My lips are parched."

"We can't have parched lips," he agreed with a chuckle as he poured the tainted cider into the goblets. "You need lips that are moist and kissable."

She took the cup and pretended to drink as he drained the contents of his goblet. "This is good cider," he commented.

"Have more," Eleanore offered, refilling his goblet. She noticed that a dull, unfocused look had developed on his face as he drank the second cupful in one long gulp.

After he'd finished, he grabbed her around the waist with both hands. "You are the most *boo-ti-awful* creature I haf 'ere seen," he said, his words now badly slurred. "An' ah mus haf ye."

With surprising strength, he tossed her lightly onto the bed behind them and stood, regarding her hungrily with bleary eyes. In the next second, he lunged at her on the bed, knocking her flat against the mattress—and began to snore noisily.

Eleanore was pinned under his heavy, inert body, unable to free herself. "Sisters," she hissed, afraid to wake him. "Sisters, help!"

She heard a scuffling of feet and her sisters appeared, giggling by the bedside. "I see that he found you irresistible," Isolde teased.

"I think he's cute," Mathilde said.

"Don't be idiots," Eleanore scolded. "Roll him off me."

They were able to lift him enough so that Eleanore could slide out from underneath. He didn't even sputter as they shoved him, and they had no fear that he would awaken. Eleanore covered him with a blanket and left him there to sleep.

She put on her slippers and grabbed a lantern as the others pushed the bed aside. One by one they descended into the opening in the floor. Looking wistfully over her shoulder at Edgar, Eleanore followed them down into the dark tunnel below.

She could not stop thinking about Edgar, Lord Liddington. Although he was a nobleman, there was an earthy quality about him that had strongly appealed to her. He'd said he'd marry her too. It flattered her that she was the one he would have chosen and made her like him even more.

All thoughts of Edgar flew out of her mind, however, as they came into the glowing cavern and Morgan's enchantment once again took hold of them. Her nightgown transformed into an opulent, jeweled ball gown and her long hair twisted itself up into an elaborate coif of braids and ringlets.

The six golden barges appeared in the middle of the glittering lake and silently approached. With their minds clouded by Morgan's enchantment, the sisters welcomed the sight of the stag princes, seeing them only as dashing figures who would usher them off to a night of dancing and frolic. They were liberators, come to free the girls from the drudgery of their daily lives.

After they had enjoyed another night of fun, they

returned at dawn and cautiously approached the opening in the floor.

Isolde was at the head of the line. She raised her head over the floor, peering around the room, then she ducked it back under. "Mary is still snoring, but I don't hear Lord Liddington."

"Do you see him?" Eleanore asked.

Isolde checked. "No," she reported.

Eleanore wondered what they should do. If the sleeping potion hadn't held and Edgar had managed to rouse himself, she didn't want him to catch them coming up out of the floor—although now that the effects of the enchantment were wearing off, she realized that she wouldn't have minded entirely if that happened.

"Blow out your lights," she instructed her sisters in a low tone. "Go up quietly and check if he's still in his bed."

Nodding, they doused the lights and proceeded to climb out of the opening. Moonlight pouring through the bedchamber window made it possible for them to see where they were going.

Eleanore was just lifting herself over the floorboards when she heard Isolde's terrified yelp. She, along with her sisters, hurried to Isolde's side.

Edgar lay on the bed, flat on his back and no longer snoring. His ruddy face had grown unnaturally pale. "He's dead," Isolde whimpered.

Eleanore shoved past her and shook Edgar's shoulder violently. "Edgar!" she shouted frantically. "Wake up!"

She thumped his chest with her fists. "Wake up, Edgar!" she shouted more loudly into his ear.

When she still received no response, she jumped back, her hand over her mouth in horror.

Isolde had been right. He was dead! She'd killed him!

CHAPTER TWENTY-THREE
Rowena Objects

Rowena was standing by the bedchamber window when two man servants carried Lord Liddington out on a pallet. When they had awakened Mary and told her that the man was dead, she'd hurried off in a panic to inform Sir Ethan.

Sir Ethan had returned to the bedchamber with Mary and, upon examining Lord Liddington, determined that he still manifested a faint heartbeat.

"Thank God!" Eleanor had gasped.

Their father had looked at her sharply. "Do you know what has befallen this man?" he challenged suspiciously.

"No," Eleanore had lied quickly. "I'm just glad he lives."

"He is barely alive," Sir Ethan had grumbled. "I will bring him to rest in a spare bedchamber and summon a doctor."

"Now will you cancel this absurd contest?" Mary had asked him, wringing her hands anxiously.

"Not at all," he'd told her. "It is more important than ever before to discover what is going on in my very own home."

"Very well, sir," Mary had agreed obediently. "Shall I have the girls line up their slippers for your review?"

He glanced around the room and saw the ruined slippers scattered about just as dirty and torn up as they were every morning. "Don't even bother!" he'd grumbled angrily as he left.

Now, as the door slammed shut behind the departing servants carrying away the comatose Lord Liddington, Rowena turned toward the window. She could see Bedivere below her, gazing up at her window. A shiver ran through her as she wondered what she would have done if it had been him that they'd poisoned with their sleeping potion.

She crossed the room to where Eleanore lay on her bed, deep in thought, and sat on the end of the bed. "It's over, you know," she said.

"What's over?" Eleanore asked, propping herself up onto her elbows.

"We can't poison another man," Rowena pointed out, a note of incredulity in her voice. Wasn't this fact obvious to Eleanore?

"We didn't poison him," Chloe disagreed, joining them on the bed.

"He's just still sleeping off the effects of the potion," Helewise added as she came closer along with the remaining sisters.

"His heart was *barely* beating," Rowena reminded them. "We couldn't even see any breath coming from him."

"But he didn't die," Bronwyn insisted.

"I'll add water to the potion," Eleanore said decisively. "It will weaken it so that the next man will wake up in the morning."

"But what if he doesn't?" Rowena argued. "It's a huge risk to take."

"He will," Eleanore snapped at her irritably.

"Of course he will," Ione said, and the rest of the sisters murmured their agreement.

Rowena scowled at them angrily and returned to her own bed. What was wrong with them? How could they gamble with a man's health like that? What if they put the next man in the same sort of living death as Lord Liddington? What if they actually did kill the next man to come through?

What if the next man was Bedivere?

Just as her sisters did, Rowena knew the lure of the island, the pull to go toward it, no matter what. It was a strong urge offering the reward of instant pleasure, the powerful feeling of being attractive, and the thrill of the dance. Her sisters, though, seemed more powerfully caught in its thrall than she.

Right from the start, she'd hung back; she'd had reservations and misgivings. Perhaps, she considered, it was because her need for the things the island offered was not as great. She, of them all, was the only one who knew what it was to be kissed by a man, to feel herself desired and even loved. She did not need a fantastical stag prince to spin her around a dance floor. She would have much preferred to dance with Bedivere.

Still ... there was a need that compelled her to go with them through the trapdoor each night. She had been staring into the bowl she'd found that day in the forest, the one in which she'd seen the figure Eleanore had said was their mother.

The island had made her sisters forget about finding their mother, but she hadn't forgotten. Every time she went through that opening it was with the intention that she would not go to the island. Instead, she would search the cavern and underground passageways for her mother. But each time she got into the cavern, the enchantment would pull her like some hypnotic spell and she would forget her quest just as her sisters did.

Rowena took the bowl out from under her bed and stared into it. It began to glow. She was tempted to alert her sisters but instead she kept her concentration on the light, resolved to discover what it might reveal.

The woman appeared again.

Leaning closer, Rowena saw that she appeared to be floating, her long hair dancing at the side of her face, her gown flowing around her. She reached out and gathered together a handful of small lights. Cupping them between her hands, she reached out, presenting the twinkling lights.

The lights ... could they be ... the sparkling lights in the lake?

As the golden glow faded from the bowl, Rowena

looked up and was faced with her sisters who had been observing her curiously. "What did you see?" Brianna asked.

"I think our mother is trapped below the lake," she told them.

"For all these years?" Bronwyn questioned doubtfully.

"Wouldn't she drown?" Cecily added.

Rowena recalled what Bedivere had told her. He was searching for a magical figure in a mystical lake. "Our mother wouldn't drown if she were the Lady of the Lake," she said as the truth struck her.

"*Our* mother?" Mathilde questioned with a small laugh of disbelief. "Are you saying that *our* mother is the Lady of the Lake?"

Rowena nodded. "Yes. I have come to believe that she is."

"Has someone told you this?" Eleanore asked suspiciously.

Rowena could not tell them about Bedivere, how he sought the lady who so perfectly fit the description of their missing mother. But the more she considered it, the more certain she became. "No one has said anything to me," she lied to Eleanore, "but it makes sense. It explains why I seem to see her in water—why I am seeing her at all. She is contacting me through her magic."

"Or perhaps you are contacting her through inherited magic of your own," Bronwyn offered seriously. This sobering thought made Rowena draw in a slow, quavering breath. She supposed it was possible, recalling her visions of Bedivere.

"If that's so, how do we free her?" Brianna asked. "We swam in the lake. We even dove below the surface, and we didn't see her."

"I don't know," Rowena admitted.

At that moment Mary entered with a basket of fresh, new slippers. "How is Edgar?" Eleanore asked her eagerly.

"Who?" Mary asked.

"Lord Liddington," Eleanore explained.

Mary began distributing the slippers to each sister. "The physician has come to see the poor man. He's doubtful that Lord Liddington will awaken any time soon, if ever." She stopped and looked at them searchingly. "Girls, what happened? I was awake all night, and I didn't see or hear anything."

The sisters would have laughed at this had the situation not been so dire.

"Maybe he had an illness before he got here," Eleanore suggested.

"Well, then heaven knows what this next man will bring in with him," Mary muttered.

"What's he like?" Chloe asked.

"He's a poor, coughing madman," she told them. "Just the other day he came begging at the front gate, wanting a meal. I sent one to him, but he didn't even have the sense to wait for it."

"Why did father give *him* a number?" Brianna asked, complaining.

"He turned him down but someone must have given a ticket to him," Mary said. "You girls better hope he doesn't get to wed one of you, though I dare say that he'd be quite handsome if he wasn't such a mess."

Rowena's hand went to her throat as she realized who Mary was talking about. Bedivere! Her beloved would come in and be the next to fall prey to the poisoned goblet her sisters would insist on offering him.

Should she tell them about Bedivere, explain to them this was the man she loved more passionately than life itself?

She waited for Mary to leave and then spoke to her sisters. "You cannot hurt this man," she insisted. "It's wrong!"

"What's he to you?" Eleanore asked. The subject seemed to make her irritable now and her voice was sharp.

"I have seen him from the window," she said cautiously, still deciding how much to tell. "He seems like a good man."

"What did he do, wink at you and win your heart?" Chloe teased.

"And what if he did?" Rowena replied.

"The beggar?" Mathilde questioned.

"A person's fortunes may rise or fall as the wheel of fate spins," Rowena answered. "But a person's character remains constant."

Eleanore got off her bed and approached Rowena in a bullying, dominant manner that Rowena didn't care for. "I will dilute the potion as I said I would, but I will not have some beggar exposing our nightly pleasures to our father."

"And what if I tell him where we go?" Rowena countered boldly.

"If that is your intention I will tie you up and shove you in the closet," Eleanore threatened.

"Let's not fight," Isolde intervened. "Rowena, the man will be all right. Eleanore will dampen the potion and he will awake in the morning as he should."

Rowena walked toward the window and gazed out. If she did reveal their secret to Bedivere, their father would seal up the opening and she would have no chance of searching for their mother.

There was a possibility that her father might take up the search himself. But what if he didn't believe her?

She wished she could be sure of what to do, but at the moment her mind spun with indecision.

CHAPTER TWENTY-FOUR
Bedivere Takes His Turn

Bedivere tied a hammock he'd made from a discarded horse blanket between two trees, and tried to sleep. He managed to slumber for brief moments, but he was too anxious to give in to completely unconscious sleep. He had to know if the first man to enter, a strapping, well-dressed fellow, would come out of the manor.

At dawn he opened his eyes and saw a physician entering through the front gate with a servant from the house. He worried that something had happened to Rowena and could sleep no more. He began to glance anxiously up at the window for a sign of Rowena but didn't see her.

The sun was well up in the sky when the physician came out of the manor. "Good doctor," Bedivere accosted the physician as he rode his horse up the trail. "What's happened?"

"The first competitor has fallen ill with a mysterious malady," the physician revealed. "He is in a comatose state, not quite dead and not quite alive."

Although Bedivere was sorry for the man, he couldn't help but feel relief. He grew eager to be called, to have his chance to see Rowena again.

Servants came out with food during the day to feed the twenty or so men who had camped out, awaiting their chance. Finally, around sunset, a man servant came to the front door and called out, "Number two!"

The servant appraised Bedivere skeptically when he stepped forward, but Bedivere handed the man his card and the servant had no choice but to admit him.

He followed the servant through elegant hallways on the first floor until they came to the part of the house made of hand-hewn beams and wooden floors, an older part of the manor that obviously pre-dated the rest. Bedivere took note of this as well as of every other detail of the manor. He didn't yet know what information would prove valuable to him in this quest, and his training as a knight had taught him to mark the details of each new location carefully.

Mary met him and the servant outside the bedchamber. She delivered a stern warning against any improper advances on the sisters. "You are simply to report what you discover," she instructed. "Take no action."

Bedivere nodded and waited as she unbolted the door. His heart raced at the thought that in seconds he would see her.

And then, quickly, he was inside the bedchamber faced with twelve curious young women. His gaze darted from one to the other, searching, until he came to Rowena and he smiled at her with his eyes.

She returned his warm gaze but was cut short by Mary's sharp voice. "This is Bedivere of . . ."

". . . of the North Country," he supplied politely.

Mary cast a disapproving eye on him. "Yes . . . very well . . ." The servants came in with the towels, pitcher, and basin as they had the night before. "You can wash up and I've taken the liberty of providing you with a new tunic, vest, and leggings from our clothing supplies," she said.

"Thanks for your kindness," he said as he followed her and the servants into the adjacent room.

Mary went out again and drew the drape shut behind her. "A wash up and new clothing should make him a bit more presentable," she told the sisters in a conspiratorial whisper that Bedivere could easily hear as he pulled his tunic over his head.

"He'll be gorgeous!" Ione stated in a loud whisper. Her comment pleased him and he began to wash, hoping Rowena would agree with her sister.

"Now I see why you like him so much," Chloe said to Rowena.

"He carries two swords," Helewise had observed. "I wonder why. The one in the scabbard on his belt is quite spectacular."

"Did you notice that his left hand doesn't move?" Eleanore commented. "It's been injured in some way."

Rowena shushed her harshly, but it was too late. Bedivere had heard this last comment, and it made him acutely self-conscious of his defect. He looked down at his useless hand, hoping Rowena did not find it as repugnant as the distaste in Eleanore's voice implied.

He finished washing and dressed in the new clothes, leaving his sword and Excalibur lying on the bed. He pulled open the drape and gazed about the bedchamber. The sisters stared at him with such frank admiration that it made him nearly forget his insecurity over his hand.

He noticed that Mary was speaking to someone through the locked door. She felt his gaze on her and turned. "The door is now bolted from the outside," she told him. "The windows do not open. There is no way out." She pointed to the silken slippers parked under each sister's bed. "Can you tell me how these slippers are being destroyed each night?"

"No, I can't," he admitted, "but by morning I hope I will be able to explain it to you."

He realized that Rowena was looking at him intently as if trying to convey some message. He raised his eyebrows quizzically and, with a nearly imperceptible nod of her head, she indicated that he should step back into his room.

He did this, drawing the drape closed. He waited, not knowing what she wanted him to do next.

"Stay inside, sir," Mary called to him. "The girls will be changing into their nightclothes."

"I'll stay put," he agreed loudly.

He sat on the bed and shut his eyes, excited by the nearness of her, the knowledge that she was right next door.

Out of a slit between the drape and the doorway, he saw Rowena's back as she inched slowly toward his room. He stood to be closer to her. "Drink nothing," she whispered without turning around.

CHAPTER TWENTY-FIVE
Morgan Gets Serious

The tiny mouse sat under the knight's bed and exulted in her good fortune. Excalibur was sitting on the bed above her at this very moment. The most powerful magic weapon ever created had been hand delivered to her.

It was really just too good!

Morgan the mouse leaned up against the carved leg of the narrow bed and pressed her side into a curve of the wood to itch her wound. The sword certainly delivered a nasty gash. She'd never intended to fight Bedivere, having learned from their last battle how overpowering Excalibur was. She'd just lost her temper when he'd refused to accept the bribe she'd offered.

He was so disgustingly noble!

And smart, too, as it turned out. The fortune she'd offered him would have turned to sawdust the moment she had disappeared with Excalibur. The ticket also would have disintegrated right in his hand.

It would have been satisfying for her to see him realize he'd been made a fool of, he who was making this so impossibly difficult for her. If he had just left the sword next to the dead Arthur, she could have picked it up from the battlefield and never have had to turn into these ignominious forms or incurred these injuries in pursuit of it.

None of it mattered anymore.

Soon Eleanore would bring in a cup of poisoned cider. Good Sir Bedivere would drink it and fall asleep, never knowing what had hit him. That clod Mary would fall asleep on her own, and the girls would disappear down their hole in the floor.

All that remained was for Morgan to change out of this horrid mouse shape, pluck up Excalibur, and transport out of the room with it. Easy!

"Got ya!" Bedivere's hand came down and scooped her up, holding her loosely in his closed palm. He opened his hand slightly and peered in at her. "I've no food here for you," he said gently, though to her large sensitive ears his words banged painfully like thunder.

"Come back in the morning, though, and I'll share my breakfast."

She scrambled from his hand, needing to escape the unbearable loudness of his voice. He'd said he was going to do something in the morning; she'd understood that much. *You'll be as good as dead in the morning,* she thought, scurrying through a crack under the floor.

Safely in the darkness below the floor, she wondered what she should do about Vivienne and her daughters. Now that she would soon have Excalibur in hand, it might be time to do away with them altogether.

Yes, it was, most definitely.

The magic in Excalibur would give her the power to kill Vivienne, a thing she had previously lacked.

And with an adjustment in her magical incantation, the enchanted island, along with the stag princes, could become something much more perilous than a seductive addiction. The island could turn dangerous, and the stag princes might manifest, quite unexpectedly, a darker, more deadly side of their animal natures.

This night would be as good a time as any to unleash the wild beasts of her new powers.

CHAPTER TWENTY-SIX
Bedivere Finds His Way

The lights in the bedchamber went out and soon Bedivere heard snoring coming from the serving woman's bed. He had kept his lamp lit and, by the dim light it shed into the next room, he could see a female figure in a nightgown approaching him.

He dared to hope it was Rowena, but it was her sister who pushed aside the half-drawn drapery and entered his sleeping area carrying two goblets and a jug. It amazed him that she could look so much like Rowena and yet emanate none of her warmth or sensual spark. "I thought we might share a drink," she offered a bit stiffly.

Instantly, he remembered Rowena's warning. "I thank you," he said courteously, "but might I request to share it with Rowena? It is she I will ask to wed if I can unravel this puzzle."

"How do you know her name?" she asked sharply.

"She told it to me . . . in a dream," he replied.

She eyed him suspiciously as she set the goblets and jug by the basin on the night stand and went out. He heard the sisters engage in some urgent, argumentative whispering in the bedchamber before the drape was pushed aside again and, this time, Rowena did step into the room.

In seconds she was in his arms and they were kissing with desperate passion. She pulled back from him, holding up one finger for a pause. She stood close to the drape and spoke more loudly than she might have otherwise for the benefit of her sisters. "Let me pour you a cup of cider."

She motioned for him to reply with a wave of her hand. "Oh ... yes ... that would be good," he said, getting her message.

She filled the goblet and he reached out to take it from her, but she shook her head. Crouching, she poured the liquid carefully into a groove between two floorboards. "Here, have another," she said in the same overly loud voice.

His eyes widened with alarm as he suddenly understood what had happened to his predecessor. These sisters were poisoning each man in order to keep their secret safe.

Rowena sat on the bed and indicated that he should sit close beside her. Glad to oblige he came next to her, encircling her with his arm. She leaned close and spoke into his ear in a barely audible whisper. "Do not drink this cider for any reason. When I leave, pretend to be in a sleep from which nothing can rouse you, but listen for movement in my bedchamber. Follow us with the greatest stealth and bring both of your swords."

"Are you willing for me to know the secret your father wishes me to uncover?" he asked.

She looked away from him uneasily as though she didn't know the answer to that. Then she turned back to him with a new determination. "I wish you to find the lake that you seek. I believe I can lead you to it. Perhaps when you find it you will also find my mother who has been missing since I was a child."

"I seek Arthur's kinswoman, the Lady of the Lake," he whispered back, not understanding her.

She gazed into his eyes and nodded.

"Your mother is that lady?" he asked.

"I've come to believe so."

"What shall I report to your father?"

A movement in the drape told him that someone was outside and he put his finger to his lip to caution her. "It seems, fair maiden, that I am overcome with a powerful fatigue I cannot explain."

"Sleep then, sir," Rowena said to him as she got off the bed. "I look forward to seeing you in the morning."

"But I must stay awake to learn your secret," he feigned a protest.

"Sleep," she insisted as he crawled under the covers and closed his eyes, pretending to be out cold. "Sleep is what you need."

He heard her pull back the drape. "What have you been doing all this time?" one of the sisters demanded in an angry whisper. It sounded to him like the sister who had first come in.

"No need to whisper," Rowena said to her. "He is completely asleep thanks to the potion."

The other sister stepped into the room and moved the goblets. "Well, I see one of them has been used and is now empty," she noted, her suspicion seemingly satisfied. "I didn't think you would go through with it."

"I told you I would," Rowena replied. "Now let's go."

Observing them through slitted eyes as they moved away, he saw balls of light spring to life in their bedchamber. He heard something heavy, maybe a bed, being pushed aside. There was grunting as the sisters exerted a great effort to open something that had a creaky hinge.

As a youth training to be a knight, he'd been schooled in the practice of stealth. He'd been taught to sneak up on an enemy while wearing chain mail and armor, and so he did not find it difficult now to strap on Excalibur, slide his sword into his belt, slip into his boots, and follow the sisters soundlessly down through the trapdoor.

He kept far back, concentrating on the last pinpoint of dim light in their procession through the tunnel. He made sure not to lose sight of the light, though, fearing that the intense darkness would engulf him if he did.

So intense was his concentration that only after several yards did he become aware of the rhythm of drums and flutes surrounding him. It reminded him of his boyhood in the hills of the north and he remembered dancing with his sisters on the heather-purple moors. Liveliness crept into his step and he resisted the urge to turn a jig, thinking it would be too ridiculous a thing to do under his current circumstances. Still, the very idea of it caused him to smile.

After a while he could see a soft whitish green glow in the distance, as though the tunnel would come out to a tremendous room illuminated with this gentle light.

Hurrying, he arrived at the cavern in time to see six golden barges gliding away from the shore on the surface of a lake alive with sparkling lights. Strange animal-men with antlers stood aboard the barges beside the sisters, who were now, somehow, extravagantly attired.

He spotted Rowena at the back of one of the barges, her beauty magnified by the splendor of her dress and hair. Completely smitten as he was with her already, he had never imagined that her considerable loveliness could be further elevated so that she appeared to be no less than a princess. But there she was, the most intoxicatingly beautiful sight he'd ever seen.

And then she was gone as the barges turned behind a rocky outcropping and disappeared from view.

He slumped against a boulder, angry at himself for letting them get away from him. In the next second, though, he realized that he had finally come to the shores of a lake.

He observed the lights sparkling just above and below its surface. This was what Rowena had wanted him to find!

Unsheathing Excalibur, he waved it above his head.

A low, vibrating hum echoed off the cavern's high rock walls as the surface of the lake was suddenly covered in blinding light.

CHAPTER TWENTY-SEVEN
Morgan the Bat

The mouse opened one drugged eye as she lay on her side on the dirt beneath the floorboards. Twitching her whiskers, she peered into the darkness.

Ow! She felt as if her head had been smashed with a skillet!

As she lay there blinking her way back to consciousness, she remembered having run under the floor to escape Bedivere's banging gong of a voice. She'd been standing under there, waiting for all of them to leave, planning their final destruction, when a sweet liquid had come trickling down on her head.

All she'd done was lick some off her fur to find out what it was and—lights out! It was the last thing she remembered doing.

What shameful ignominy—to be laid flat by her own poisonous concoction! Why on Earth had someone poured it into the floor?

Staggering to her furry feet, she listened. Someone out there was snoring like a thunderstorm.

Although even the slightest movement caused her head to feel as though it might explode, Morgan crept slowly out from under the floor. Her mouse vision enabled her to see easily in the dark as she scurried into the bedchamber.

The trapdoor was open. The heavily slumbering Mary was the only one still there! Bedivere was gone, too, and it seemed he'd taken Excalibur with him!

Why would he do that unless Rowena had figured out that her mother was the lady he sought and had told him he could find her in the underground lake?

Morgan didn't know what might happen if that sword intersected with the magic of the lake. The lake might act on it like an accelerator, multiplying its power many times over. It was certainly possible.

She turned back into herself, which lessened the pain in her head slightly. There was no time to be wasted now. She had to get down into the underground cavern and stop Bedivere from throwing Excalibur into the lake.

As she began to lower herself into the opening, she stumbled on the first step. She'd never catch up with them like this and becoming a mouse might be even slower. Making time was essential now.

A look of determined concentration came over her as she shifted shape and changed into a bat. With a flourish of leathery wings, she swooped down into the tunnel.

CHAPTER TWENTY-EIGHT
Vivienne's Chance

Vivienne gazed up slowly as the surface of the lake above her began to shine. It was only a shard of light at first, but it rapidly grew until the entire watery roof above her head was ablaze.

She knew that hum, had heard it many times in the course of her training in magic. The last time it had vibrated so intensely was when she created the magic from which Excalibur was formed.

Excalibur!

It was the only thing in the world that could make the magical energies of the universe reverberate at such a speed!

What was happening?

Swimming with all her strength, she made it to the surface and pushed against the bubble-like covering just below the light. It pushed back, but she could tell that it wasn't as strong as it had been. The magical light over it was weakening its power.

Vivienne centered all her physical strength and pushed again. Her right arm blasted through the seal, pushed up through the light.

"Come to me!" she shouted to Excalibur, her arm stretched to its limit, her hand spread wide, ready and waiting for it to be delivered.

There was a whistling in the air as the sword was thrown across the lake. It turned end over end and then—

She caught it!

With an ecstatic cry of triumph, she swung it in a circle three times before pulling it below the surface.

Sinking to the bottom of the lake, clutching the sword to her, she gazed at its magnificence. She had imbued it with all the powerful magic at her command, and now it had come back to her with its power intact. She pressed her cheek against the flat of its blade and allowed its invigorating magic to surge through her body, restoring her to new strength.

Pushing off from the floor of the lake she surged upward, this time bursting completely through the magical seal over the lake as she rose in a spray of water. Her joy at being free was so great that it acted as a field of energy that allowed her to hover there in the air.

She expected to see her daughters there on the shore but was surprised to see instead a strapping, handsome man staring at her, wide-eyed with surprise. She had seen his face before in her dream of Arthur's death on the battlefield. He had sat beside her dying nephew, talking with him consolingly.

Vivienne noticed something else. There was a bat circling above his head.

Chapter Twenty-nine
Bedivere Disappears

The shimmering apparition that had been hanging in the air above the lake suddenly appeared by Bedivere's side. "You have done me a great service," the stately woman said to him. "I thank you."

"I did it at the bidding of my king and friend, Arthur, your nephew," he told her.

Bedivere noticed that, although she looked at him, she was also checking something above his head. Following the direction of her gaze, he saw the bat for the first time. It sat high up on one of the rock ledges, observing them with its red eyes.

"How did you find this lake?" she asked him.

He quickly told her of his strange connection with Rowena. "She is your soul mate," Vivienne told him, nodding with understanding. "Because of her heightened abilities, she was able to connect with you at your time of great distress. She did it without even trying because her heart is open to these natural currents. You made contact with one another because, in the same way, you too are an open-hearted soul."

He went on to tell her everything that had happened. She became concerned when he told her how he had seen her twelve daughters depart on golden barges, disappearing around the turn in the lake.

"This bears the marks of enchantment," she commented to him. "It worries me. Let us go to them immediately." Laying Excalibur at her feet, she spread her arms over it and it became a luminous sailboat aboard which they both stepped.

Bedivere took hold of its rudder but the boat took off on its own, sailing toward the outcropping in the lake. Vivienne looked up as the bat flew over their heads, quickly getting ahead of them.

The lake grew choppy, tossing the boat. "It's as I suspected," Vivienne told him as she clung to the boat's sides. "That bat is an evil spirit. It might even be Morgan le Fey, the one who first trapped me here. If it is she who has worked this enchantment on them, they are in great danger indeed."

She lifted her arms, mysteriously moving the sailboat to the shore of the enchanted island. A horrified scream caused Bedivere to pivot toward its source. Rowena was being chased by a creature that was dressed as the stag princes had been clothed but who had become part bull and part dragon. This creature had grabbed Rowena, and Bedivere couldn't tell if it was trying to press its unwanted lust upon her or to devour her. Eleven other creatures like that one pursued her sisters.

Bedivere was about to lunge off the side of the boat and swim to the island. Vivienne clutched his arm to stop him. Reaching into the boat, she pulled up a cloak and tossed it to Bedivere. "Being a mortal, you cannot go where I will now take you. Put this on so no one will see you there. If you love Rowena, stay hidden from her until the time is right."

Putting on the cloak, he became instantly invisible.

Vivienne went to the bow of the sailboat and raised her arms. As she brought them down sharply, the scene abruptly changed.

CHAPTER THIRTY
Princess Rowena

All at once the creature that had been about to sink its fanged teeth into Rowena's neck disappeared. She found that she was suddenly sitting in the middle of a ring of very tall, vertical, rectangular stones that stood straight up and which were connected by similarly large stones at the top. Once again, she was dressed in her nightgown and slippers.

She was relieved to have escaped the enchanted island, where everything had suddenly turned ugly— the stag princes changed to monsters, the food rotted, the music dissolved to discordant clanging—at the very moment a disgusting little bat had landed on a table. Although she was thankful to have been whisked away from that horrible scene, she was completely confused now.

Her sisters appeared inside the stone rings, also dressed in their nightgowns and slippers once again.

A lovely woman with long, blond hair was the last to appear among them. She stood by a tall slab regarding them warmly. Rowena slowly recognized her from the vision in the scrying bowl as her own mother, Vivienne, the Lady of the Lake.

"Mother!" Mathilde cried, the next to realize who she was. She ran to the woman and threw her arms around her. Rowena joined several more of her sisters as they surrounded the woman.

Only Eleanore hung back. "Where have you been?" she demanded. "What became of you? Why did you abandon us?"

"My dearest daughter," the woman replied kindly. "I would never willingly have left you." She explained to them everything that had happened including how Morgan le Fey had enthralled them with the diversions of the island in order to distract them from finding her.

As she finished her story, their faces were wet with tears, partly from sadness and partly from their extreme joy at having their mother returned to them. Even Eleanore cried with mixed emotions.

"Enough of tears," Vivienne told them as she hugged each one. "We are together here at the great stone ring, the most special of all places to the people of Avalon, and summer begins this night! The people will be arriving soon, and they will see you reunited with me, their queen, as the great princesses of Avalon that you have become."

Majestically lifting one hand, she changed their nightgowns into elegantly simple, diaphanous, flowing gowns and caused circlets of wildflowers and leaves to appear around their heads.

The type of music that they'd heard in the tunnels was now amplified many fold with the banging of drums, the melody of flutes, and the strumming of harps filling the circle. From between the spaces separating the stones stepped sorcerers and sorceresses, the mystical inhabitants of the magical island of Avalon.

After they rejoiced to see Vivienne and her daughters, all of them danced in a circle, moving rhythmically to the music. The sisters joined the dance, their feet moving as though they had always done the steps.

The dancing continued until the first line of sunlight rose above the horizon and painted a shining line of vertical light on one of the slabs. The dancing citizens of Avalon walked toward the line of sunlight and, one by one, disappeared into it.

Rowena looked to Vivienne for direction. "Go through," she instructed her daughters. "I will join later. I must go to Avalon before returning to you. Rest assured that I will follow."

Rowena was the first to step into the vertical line of sunlight. Once again she was back on the enchanted island, though now it was nothing but an empty island. The sailboat Vivienne had arrived in, sat on the shore.

Rowena climbed into it, feeling that her mother had left it there for her safe return. As each of her sisters appeared, they boarded the boat.

They were all aboard when Rowena noticed a rocking in the boat as though some thirteenth person had entered although no one had. It frightened her to think that some unseen spirit had come aboard with them.

The boat set sail and the presence was very close to her. She smelled a familiar pleasant scent. Was it him or merely someone wearing his clothing, trying to fool her?

Chapter Thirty-one
Bedivere Is Trapped

Bedivere wanted desperately to reveal his presence to Rowena. But Rowena had told her sisters that she'd left him behind in a drugged sleep. He didn't want to take it upon himself to reveal her lie to them.

So he stayed beneath the invisibility cloak, concealed from sight. As they sailed along, he enjoyed the nearness of her. He couldn't resist the temptation to reach out while still covered with the cloak and lay his good hand on top of hers as she rested it on the side of the boat.

She raised her head, alarmed by his touch and peered at him so keenly that he could almost swear that she saw him. "Who is there?" she whispered.

He squeezed her hand to reassure her. Again, her eyes bore into his, confused, yet somehow seeming to sense it was him. She opened her mouth to speak but was distracted by a dark, winged form swooping above the boat.

"There's that bat," she told her sisters, pointing to it. "Why is it flying above us? I'm afraid it might be a witch or evil spirit. It appeared on the island when everything became ugly."

"That's true," Eleanore agreed. "I saw it too. Watch it closely and don't let it get too near our boat. Throw something at it if it comes too close."

Bedivere watched the bat closely as it flew along with the sailing boat. Vivienne had been concerned about it, and it had been on the island. He felt sure it was an evil presence and was glad he was there to protect the sisters should someone attempt to harm them.

He became intensely alert, on guard for any sign of danger. He recalled how he'd been attacked by something in the shape of a rock soldier and then in the shape of a wealthy man. Whomever this foe turned out to be, it could take many forms.

The boat was trailing along the shore now, and Bedivere noticed a shape bending into the water ahead of them. Sharpening his focus to see better in the dim light, he realized it was just a rotted tree that had fallen toward the lake.

But how could a tree even grow in this underground place, completely devoid of sunlight?

Something was not right.

The bat settled on the trunk of the dead tree as if waiting for the boat.

Standing, Bedivere wrapped his good hand around the hilt of his sword. He noticed that Rowena was now peering along the shore as well.

The boat sailed close enough to the tree that some of its skinny, uppermost branches came close to its hull. He could see the bat's red eyes boring into him, as though the creature knew he was there, even through his invisibility cloak. Then the bat moved into the tree's tangle of dead branches and seemed to disappear.

Bedivere leaned closer to study the dark, dead tree with its gnarled rotted bark and to search for the bat.

Rowena was also scanning the shore. At one point she came so close to him that they were right beside one another. "Bedivere?" she inquired in such a low tone it was almost a mere breath.

As he turned to answer her, a branch clutched at the hem of his invisibility cloak. With a quick yank, it tugged him over the side and strangely agile branches held him fast beneath the water's surface. The tree's grip was so tight that no matter how forcefully he thrashed, he could not break its hold on him.

CHAPTER THIRTY-TWO
Three Forests

Rowena instantly noticed the violent disturbance in the water. She'd felt that something or someone had been pulled past her and over the side. "Stop the boat," she called to her sisters.

"How?" Gwendolyn shouted back.

"Maybe we can turn it around," Chloe suggested, searching for a rudder but not finding one.

Rowena couldn't wait. She plunged overboard, swimming toward the churning, splashing water. She'd suspected that Bedivere was with her on the boat. She had to help him.

Diving under, she saw his disembodied leg, kicking madly. Around it, the water swirled. Gripping his leg with one hand she searched with the other until she thought she felt cloth. Tugging, she slowly saw more of him until the entire cape was removed.

She needed air and came up for a breath. The sailboat was a glimmer in the distance. There would be no help from her sisters.

On the surface she saw that the branches of the tree were holding him under the water. They'd gripped his right arm, circling it in a vine. It kept him from pulling out his sword and, since his left hand was unusable, he couldn't get to it.

Going back under, she swam to him and pulled his sword from his belt. With it, she hacked at the thick vine curled around his right arm and shoulder.

The vine was tough and difficult to cut through. As she worked, Bedivere struggled to loosen the branches, but air bubbles were escaping from his mouth. If she didn't free him soon he would drown.

Vine tendrils began sprouting from the branches, growing toward her, seeking to entrap her as they'd done with Bedivere. They caught hold of the ends of her hair, coiling it. She batted at them, yanking her hair away as she worked, but as much as she fought them, the vines persisted. If she let them snare her hair she wouldn't be able to get up for air.

Breathlessness caused her to stop working and go to the surface again. The vines held her so that she could only gulp air with her face out of the water.

When she went back under, she was in time to see Bedivere pull himself free from the weakened vine. He grabbed at the slim vines woven through her hair, snapping them as he pulled her to the surface with him.

The tree snapped its branches at them and banged on the water attempting to grab hold of them once more, but they dove down to escape it. Under the water, a powerful vine shot out and pursued them, seeming to sense their every move.

As they swam from it, Rowena spied a water-filled tunnel with an air space at the top. Remembering what her mother had told them about the many tunnels she'd created, Rowena signaled to Bedivere to follow her. They swam deeper and deeper through the winding turns until they were sure the tree no longer pursued them.

They swam out to a small grotto where the water swirled into a natural pool. They settled on the ledge that ran around its inside edge and caught their breaths. "And I thought I'd be protecting you," Bedivere said with a laugh.

She smiled at him as they kissed, holding one another tightly.

In a while they stepped out of the water and climbed stone steps. They were still underground but the cavern they had come into was very large, easily three times the size of the cavern they'd been in before. They were in a forest of odd trees whose leaves swooshed gently together, making a sort of whisper. It was light, too; a strange bronze-colored glow suffused everything.

"How can there be plant life without sunlight?" Bedivere questioned cautiously.

These were no ordinary trees, Rowena realized. "They're bronze," she pointed out to him.

They walked through this bronze forest watching carefully for any new form of enchanted attack, but soon they began to relax and talk.

As they spoke to one another, Rowena felt an

unexpected sadness creep over her. The melancholy appeared to have affected Bedivere as well for his words were full of missed opportunities and misgivings.

"Where do I go now that Camelot is gone?" he wondered aloud. "I have left my armor behind and will never don it again. How could I fight for another king? I have no idea how I will live and so cannot even ask for your hand in marriage."

"It doesn't matter to me," Rowena said, wrapping her hand around his arm. "I have known every luxury, and it hasn't made me happy. My life has been spent in a prison. And now that I have found my mother, now that you have freed her, she has gone away to Avalon, and I don't know where that is. You cannot leave me in that house trapped forever like a singing bird in a cage. Before I knew you I could hardly bear it. Now that we have kissed, I will forever long to kiss you again."

The thought of going back to her former life without Bedivere overpowered her with grief. She stopped walking as bitter tears flowed down her cheeks.

He put his arms around her tenderly as she sobbed into his chest. When her crying subsided she noticed that ahead of them the trees were different. Silver bushes like juniper grew about six feet tall creating high silver pathways for them to follow.

Bedivere kept his arm around her shoulder as they walked by the silver bushes. "Don't cry," he said, comforting her. "I should not have upset you with my hopeless rantings. We will be together from now on no matter what it takes."

A new wave of hopefulness swept over her at these words. "Always together from now on," she echoed loving the sound of these words.

"We could go back to the North, I suppose. My family is still there, I believe, and my father is getting older so he might welcome some help with his sheep," he went on.

"It sounds wonderful," she said sincerely. "I can spin and wouldn't mind doing it if there was some purpose for it rather than just idle women's activity." She laughed. "Don't ask me to embroider, though. I'm hopeless at it."

He smiled and held her tighter. "I never noticed a lot of embroidery going on in my household. It's beautiful there, you know. I think you'll like it."

"I think I will too."

They hugged, suddenly overflowing with joy, feeling as though all their unhappiness was behind them. Rowena noticed that the trees surrounding them were now golden, like graceful birch trees but with leaves that shimmered like coins and jingled when they moved.

She plucked one of the golden leaves. "Isn't it lovely," she commented, handing it to him. The leaf tumbled from his grasp, but he snapped it up with his other hand.

The moment he'd done it, they stared at one

another in shock. "Your hand," she said softly.

"My hand," he repeated as he turned it. He balled it into a fist and then stretched the fingers back out wide.

They faced one another with expressions of disbelief and excitement. "I don't know how, but in some way you've brought this about," he said.

"Maybe it's this place," she suggested.

"Oh, it doesn't matter," he said lifting her and spinning her happily. "It only matters that we are together."

CHAPTER THIRTY-THREE
Encounters

Morning light bathed Sir Ethan as he stared at the opened trapdoor in his daughters' bedchamber. He remembered digging this root cellar himself so many years ago. This room had been a pantry behind the kitchen back then.

Why was it open now? It made no sense to him. And yet it must have something to do with the fact that his daughters were gone.

He paced agitatedly. He no longer cared *where* they had gone. The more pressing question now was, *Why had they not returned?*

Memories of the evening Vivienne did not return flooded him. It was the possibility of this happening to his daughters that had driven him to build high walls and install thick bolts. This one thing that he had worked so hard to guard against had happened after all!

Where were his daughters?

He felt as though he would lose his mind if they did not return in the next second.

Had that beggar harmed them somehow? He would hunt him down and kill him!

Mary came to his side wringing her hands. "I cannot tell you how sorry I am, sir," she apologized for the tenth time. "I must have shut my eyes for just a second."

"Mary, they were getting out anyway," he replied. "It's the fact that they've not returned that has me half crazy."

Mary crouched by the opening and peered down. "Girls, are you down there?" she called.

"Why would they be in a root cellar?" he snapped.

"I don't know," she admitted, glancing up at him. "I'll go have a look, though."

As Mary descended into the opening, the physician who had come to see Lord Liddington entered, looking quite excited. "The man is awake!" he announced.

"What ailed him?" Sir Ethan asked in a desultory voice.

The physician went to the area where Lord Liddington had slept and picked up the jug and sniffed it.

"Help yourself to some," Sir Ethan offered.

"I think not," the physician declined emphatically. "From what Lord Liddington has told me, your girls tried to kill him with this concoction."

Sir Ethan stared at him, aghast. "That's not possible."

"I'm afraid it is," said Lord Liddington from the doorway. His blond hair was disheveled and his skin had grown sallow, but he moved under his own power. "I feel as though I drank a barrel of ale all by myself, but I am thankful to be alive."

At that moment Mary's shrieks sounded from down in the root cellar. "Get away! Get away!"

The men moved to the opening just as a large black bat flew up out of it. Thinking fast, Lord Liddington whisked a sheet from one of the beds and, using it as a net, snapped the bat up in it. The bat flapped frantically, getting out of the man's grasp. But, with the sheet still over it, it couldn't see and smashed itself into the wall. With a thud, it fell to the ground.

Still flapping her hands over her head to ward off the bat, Mary came out of the opening. Sir Ethan assured her that the bat had been captured. "Sir, that is the largest root cellar I have ever seen," she said. "It goes on and on and on. It's more like a tunnel leading to who knows where. I stopped exploring when that wretched bat swooped past me. Besides, the further I went, the darker it was; it was getting black as tar in there."

Sir Ethan thought of his missing lanterns. He had accused the servants of taking them, but now it suddenly made sense. The girls were using them in this tunnel that somehow appeared under his home. "Mary, get us three lanterns," he commanded. "Doctor, Lord Liddington, we must go down there and find my daughters."

Lanterns in hand, they were about to descend into the opening when Sir Ethan heard female voices approaching from below. "Girls!" he thundered. Though he tried to sound stern, the catch of pure relief in his voice ruined the effect.

"Father!" Eleanore was at the head of the group and she ran to him. "I'm sure you're very angry, and I'm sorry we have worried you, but please listen to what we have to tell you."

Such a mix of emotions—anger, joy, curiosity, tenderness—arose within him that he was speechless. He walked back into the room and sat on a bed as his daughters, dressed in gowns he'd never seen before, climbed up through the trapdoor. Rowena was last to come up, and behind her was Bedivere.

He listened with rapt attention as they told him everything that had happened, including all they'd discovered about their mother. "We couldn't get here before dawn because we were searching for Bedivere and Rowena."

"We tried to turn the sailboat around but we couldn't," Gwendolyn picked up the story. "Once it let us off on shore we went back to find them on foot. They had gotten lost in some very strange place, and it took them hours and hours to find their way back, but as soon as we found one another, we came straight back."

"You say you were bothered by a spirit disguised as a bat?" Mary asked, casting an eye on the creature in the sheet that was still on the floor.

They all stared at the lump underneath. Sir Ethan picked a pillow off the bed and stepped toward it. If it wasn't dead already, it soon would be.

As he knelt, intent on smothering the bat, he was aware of someone standing behind him. Turning, he looked up into two blue eyes he remembered well. Vivienne had come silently into the room.

"You don't need to do that," she said. She held a thick glass box in which she put the unconscious bat. "I brought this from Avalon. It will keep her from spiriting away, and she will be tried in Avalon for her crimes."

"Vivienne," he said, overcome by the sight of her.

"I'm home," she replied.

His face clouded with anger as he stood. "Is that so? Just like that—you're home? Do you mind telling me where you've been? I suppose you've made a new life for yourself, have a new home, a new husband." He turned his back on her, struggling to control his emotions.

She ran her hand along his arm as she had those many years ago when they first met in the lake. "This is my only home. You are my only husband," she said gently. "I have done nothing all these years but try to return to you. I will tell you everything that has happened, but be assured that my only thought has been of you and my twelve princesses."

She drew him around to face her, and as he looked into her fathomless blue eyes he knew he could not let suspicion or mistrust interfere with the gift of her return. In truth, in the deepest, most hidden regions of his heart, he had never stopped hoping for her eventual return.

"I knew you would come," he murmured in a gruff, emotion-filled voice as she laid her cheek on his chest.

EPILOGUE

With the return of Vivienne, Sir Ethan no longer lived in terrifying fear that his daughters would also leave him. The bolts were knocked off all the interior doors and replaced with delicate hooks for purposes of privacy only. The opening in the floor, however, was boarded shut. Now that the girls had free access to come and go, there was no need for it, and no one wanted to risk any odd enchanted things coming up to bother them.

Rowena and Bedivere were married, although Vivienne told them that in the eyes of Avalon they were already husband and wife. "You went through the mystical grove that connects soul mates at the most profound level," she said. "In the bronze forest you shared your sadness and helped one another through it. When you passed that, you looked to the future together. It is the silver grove of hope. In the golden forest you experienced the complete happiness of being together."

"Did its magic heal my hand?" Bedivere asked.

"True love experienced in the golden forest heals everything," Vivienne told him.

The wedding was to be a lavish event with half of Glastonbury invited. Bedivere and Rowena went into the town to seek the children who had brought Bedivere to his sleeping mat and shared their last potato with him. They searched up and down the beggar's alley, leaving behind food they had brought in a basket.

They found the children by the town well, crying. Their mother had died of smallpox. They were crying from hunger since there was now no one to provide even one potato.

Rowena and Bedivere looked at one another. Was there a place in their life together for these children? Nodding, they answered the unspoken question that had been on both of their minds. Taking the boy and girl by the hand they brought them back to the manor.

It was while they were walking down the road with the children that they met Brother Louis. When he saw Bedivere, he was elated. "Come back to the monastery with me," he cried. "I am holding a trunk for you there. A messenger came by with it. He asked if I knew a one-handed knight. I remembered your infirmity, but I had no idea where to find you. I said I would try to find you, and here you are. Marvelous!"

At the monastery, they opened the large trunk that someone had packed with finely made clothing, books, boots, and many other things Bedivere had owned when he lived in Camelot. In it, too, was a pouch of gold coins he had been given by the many people he had aided with his knightly skills. He split the coins into two piles and gave half to the monk. "Keep the coins for the monastery and give the clothing to the poor, for I have no desire to be reminded of my old life. Those days are gone. In return, tell anyone who asks that I have joined your monastery and will have nothing to do with the outside world."

"As you wish," Brother Louis agreed. He handed Bedivere a large envelope. "The messenger said to give you this as well."

It was a letter written by Arthur before his death. In it, he bequeathed to Sir Bedivere land in North Wales. "You'll like this," he told Rowena. "It's by Llyn Dinas, a beautiful lake. Arthur and I once fought a giant there, and he knew it was very close to my father's land. At that time the wizard Merlin was with us and he hid a treasure by a nearby hill. I wonder . . ." A thoughtful look came over his face as he studied the map enclosed with the letter.

On the day of the wedding, Bedivere gave Rowena a gift, a bouquet of bronze, silver, and gold made from pieces of the forest that he had picked along the way and kept hidden in the pockets of the tunic Mary had given him that night. "Your mother says this bouquet will never die, like my love for you," he told her.

Bedivere had a regal wedding outfit made and was shockingly handsome on the day of his wedding. The children, Amren and Evanola, walked down the aisle ahead of the bride, strewing flowers in her path as she followed on the arm of Sir Ethan.

Vivienne sat on the side surrounded by many friends and kinsfolk from Avalon that the sisters would meet for the first time at the party. She and Ethan had decided that they would go to Avalon to live together for the rest of their days. This decision was based on the fact that though she could not give Ethan immortality, the magic on Avalon would extend his life for many, many years—and they had so much time to catch up on.

The party was the best anyone had ever seen. Eleanore danced every dance in the arms of Lord Liddington, who had forgiven her for nearly killing him when she had explained that it had been an accident, "in a way." She'd only meant to render him unconscious.

At the end of the wedding party, Sir Ethan announced that he would be leaving with Vivienne, though they most certainly would be in touch. Any of the girls who wanted to come with them and study mystical ways were welcome. "You are princesses in Avalon," Vivienne reminded them in an attempt at gentle persuasion.

Rowena declined, saying that she and Bedivere were headed for Wales. Eleanore also said no. Edgar, Lord Liddington, had hinted that he had a castle he'd like her to consider running as his wife.

Gwendolyn, Helewise, Chloe, Isolde, and Mathilde thought life on Avalon sounded exciting, though.

"Could Ione, Brianna, Bronwyn, Cecily, and I stay here at the manor?" asked Ashlynn.

"Yes, I suppose so," Sir Ethan agreed. "I'll insist that you keep the servants on for your safety."

"Oh, we'll need them, especially Helen and Mary," Ashlynn told him, "because we'd like to turn the place into an inn."

There was a murmur of approval as this seemed like it would be a fun enterprise. It turned out to be as good an idea as they thought. Even though only five of the sisters actually ran it, they named it the Inn of the Twelve Dancing Princesses.

And each sister, in her own way, went on to live exciting, happy lives. But most ecstatic of all was Rowena with her knightly, chivalrous, kind shepherd husband and their two adopted children.

Thanks to the unearthed treasure of Merlin, neither they nor anyone in the Welsh town, with which they generously shared it all, ever wanted for anything ever again.

Sir Bedivere sometimes told the local children tales of Sir Arthur and the knights of the Round Table. When he did, he did not think of the bloody warfare or the despair he'd known. He remembered, instead, the thrilling adventure, the bravery and nobility. And if a note of sadness ever crept into his voice, he would look up to see Rowena standing nearby and he would remember how she had connected with him on the battlefield—how she had saved his life that day and forever after.

About the Author

SUZANNE WEYN loved researching and imagining life in the fifth century. She learned much about the legends of King Arthur, Morgan le Fey, the Lady of the Lake, and Sir Bedivere—studying their historical roots and mythical variations. Melding these myths with the age-old fairy tale "The Twelve Dancing Princesses" was a joyful labor because the tale—though well-loved from her childhood for its exotic, mysterious nature—always seemed to her to need another narrative piece. Inventing that piece was pure pleasure.

Suzanne is also the author of *South Beach Sizzle*, written with Diana Gonzalez; *The Bar Code Tattoo*; *The Bar Code Rebellion*; and *Reincarnation*. Her Once upon a Time books include *Water Song* and *The Crimson Thread*. Visit her at SuzanneWeynBooks.com.

DON'T MISS THE NEXT MAGICAL TITLE
IN THE ONCE UPON A TIME SERIES!

BELLE
A Retelling of "Beauty and the Beast"

BY CAMERON DOKEY

Celeste. April. Belle.

Everything about my sisters and me was arranged in this fashion, in fact. It was the way our beds were lined up in our bedroom; our places at the dining table, where we all sat in a row along one side. It was the order in which we got dressed each morning and had our hair brushed for one hundred and one strokes each night. The order in which we entered a room or left it, and were introduced to guests. The only exception was when we were allowed to open our presents all together, in a great frenzy of paper and ribbons, on Christmas morning.

This may seem very odd to you, and you may wonder why it didn't to any of us. All that I can say is that order in general, but most especially the order in which one was born, was considered very important in the place where I grew up. The oldest son inherited his father's house and lands. Younger daughters did not marry unless the oldest had first walked down the aisle. So if our household paid strict attention to which sister came first, second, and (at long last) third, the truth is that none of us thought anything about the arrangement at all.

Until the day Monsieur LeGrand came to call.

Monsieur LeGrand was my father's oldest and closest friend, though Papa had seen him only once and that when he was five years old. In his own youth, Monsieur LeGrand had been the boyhood friend of Papa's father, Grand-père Georges. It was Monsieur LeGrand who had brought to Grand-mère Annabelle the sad news that her young husband had been snatched off the deck of his ship by a wave that curled around him like a giant fist, then picked him up and carried him down to the bottom of the ocean.

In some other story, Monsieur LeGrand might have stuck around, consoled the young widow in her grief, then married her after a suitable period of time. But that story is not this one. Instead, soon after reporting his sad news, Monsieur LeGrand returned to the sea, determined to put as much water as he could between himself and his boyhood home.

Eventually, Monsieur LeGrand became a merchant specializing in silk, and settled in a land where silkworms flourished, a place so removed from where he'd started out that if you marked each city with a finger on a globe, you'd need both hands. Yet even from this great distance, Monsieur LeGrand did not forget his childhood friend's young son.

When Papa was old enough, Grand-mère Annabelle took him by the hand and marched him down to the waterfront offices of the LeGrand Shipping Company. For, though he no longer lived in the place where he'd grown up, Monsieur LeGrand maintained a presence in our seaport town. My father then began the process that took him from being the boy who swept the floors and filled the coal scuttles to the man who knew as much about the safe passage of sailors and cargo as anyone.

When that day arrived, Monsieur LeGrand made Papa his partner, and the sign above the waterfront office door was changed to read LEGRAND, DELAURIER AND COMPANY. But nothing Papa ever did, not marrying Maman nor helping to bring three lovely daughers into the world, could entice Monsieur LeGrand back to where he'd started.

Over the years, he had become something of a legend in our house. The tales my sisters and I spun of his adventures were as good as any bedtime stories our nursemaids ever told. We pestered our father with endless questions to which he had no answers. All that he remembered was that Monsieur LeGrand had been straight and tall. This was not very satisfying, as I'm sure you can imagine, for any grown-up might have looked that way to a five-year-old.

Then one day—on my tenth birthday to be precise—a letter arrived. A letter that caused my father to return home from the office in the middle of the day, a thing he never does. I was the first to spot Papa, for I had been careful to position myself near the biggest of our living room windows, the better to watch for any presents that might arrive.

At first, the sight of Papa alarmed me. His face was flushed, as if he'd run all the way from the waterfront. He burst through the door, calling for my mother, then dashed into the living room and caught me up in his arms. He twirled me in so great a circle that my legs flew out straight and nearly knocked Maman's favorite vase to the floor.

He'd had a letter, Papa explained when my feet were firmly on the ground. One that was better than any birthday present he could have planned. It came from far away, from the land where the silkworms flourished, and it informed us all that, at long last, Monsieur LeGrand was coming home.

Not surprisingly, this threw our household into an uproar. For it went without saying that ours would be the first house Monsieur LeGrand would come to visit. It also went without saying that everything needed to be perfect for his arrival.

The work began as soon as my birthday celebrations were complete. Maman hired a small army of extra servants, as those who usually cared for our house were not great enough in number. They swept the floors, then polished them until they gleamed like gems. They hauled the carpets out of doors and beat them. Every single picture in the house was taken down from its place on the walls and inspected for even the most minute particle of dust. While all this was going on, the walls themselves were given a new coat of whitewash.

But the house wasn't the only thing that got polished. The inhabitants got a new shine as well. Maman was all for us being reoutfitted from head to foot, but here, Papa put his foot down. We must not be extravagant, he said. It would give the wrong impression to Monsieur LeGrand. Instead, we must provide his mentor and our benefactor with a warm welcome that also showed good sense, by which my father meant a sense of proportion.

So, in the end, it was only Papa and Maman who had new outfits from head to foot. My sisters and I each received one new garment. Celeste, being the oldest, had a new dress. April had a new silk shawl. As for me, I was the proud owner of a new pair of shoes.

It was the shoes that started all the trouble, you could say. Or, to be more precise, the buckles.

They were made of silver, polished as bright as mirrors. They were gorgeous and I loved them. Unfortunately, the buckles caused the shoes to pinch my feet, which in turn made taking anything more than a few steps absolute torture. Maman had tried to warn me in the shoe shop that this would be the case, but I had refused to listen and insisted the shoes be purchased anyhow.

"She should never have let you have your own

way in the first place," Celeste pronounced on the morning we expected Monsieur LeGrand.

My sisters and I were in our bedroom, watching and listening for the carriage that would herald Monsieur LeGrand's arrival. Celeste was standing beside her dressing table, unwilling to sit lest she wrinkle her new dress. April was kneeling on a cushion near the window, the silk shawl draped around her shoulders, her own skirts carefully spread out around her. I was the only one actually sitting down. Given the choice between the possibility of wrinkles or the guarantee of sore feet, I had decided to take my chances with the wrinkles.

But though I was seated, I was hardly sitting still. Instead, I turned my favorite birthday present and gift from Papa—a small knife for wood carving that was cunningly crafted so that the blade folded into the handle—over and over between my hands, as if the action might help to calm me.

Maman disapproves of my wood carving. She says it isn't ladylike and is dangerous. I have pointed out that I'm just as likely to stab myself with an embroidery needle as I am to cut myself with a wood knife. My mother remains unconvinced, but Papa is delighted that I inherited his talent for woodwork.

"And put that knife away," Celeste went on. "Do you mean to frighten Monsieur LeGrand?"

"Celeste," April said, without taking her eyes from the street scene below. "Not today. Stop it."

Thinking back on it now, I see that Celeste was

feeling just as nervous and excited as I was. But Celeste almost never handles things the way I do, or April either, for that matter. She always goes at things head-on. I think it's because she's always first. It gives her a different view of the world, a different set of boundaries.

"Stop what?" Celeste asked now, opening her eyes innocently wide. "I'm just saying Maman hates Belle's knives, that's all. If she shows up with one today, Maman will have an absolute fit."

"I know better than to take my wood-carving knife into the parlor to meet a guest," I said, as I set it down beside me on my dressing table.

"Well, yes, you may *know* better, but you don't always *think*, do you?" Celeste came right back. She swayed a little, making her new skirts whisper to the petticoats beneath as they moved from side to side. Celeste's new dress was a pale blue, almost an exact match for her eyes. She'd wanted it every bit as much as I'd wanted my new shoes.

"For instance, if you'd thought about how your feet might *feel* instead of how they'd *look*, you'd have saved yourself a lot of pain, and us the trouble of listening to you whine."

I opened my mouth to deny it, then changed my mind. Instead, I gave Celeste my very best smile. One that showed as many of my even, white teeth as I could. I have very nice teeth. Even Maman says so.

I gave the bed beside me a pat. "If you're so unconcerned about the way you look," I said sweetly, "why don't you come over here and sit down?"

Celeste's cheeks flushed. "Maybe I don't want to," she answered.

"And maybe you're a phony," I replied. "You care just as much about how you look as I do, Celeste. It just doesn't suit you to admit it, that's all."

"If you're calling me a liar—," Celeste began hotly.

"Be quiet!" April interrupted. "I think the carriage is arriving!"

Quick as lightning, Celeste darted to the window, her skirts billowing out behind her. I got to my feet, doing my best to ignore how much they hurt, and followed. Sure enough, in the street below, the grandest carriage I had ever seen was pulling up before our door.

"Oh, I can't see his face!" Celeste cried in frustration, as we saw a gentleman alight. A moment later, the peal of the front doorbell echoed throughout the house. April got to her feet, smoothing out her skirts as she did so. In the pit of my stomach, I felt a group of butterflies suddenly take flight.

I really did care about the way I looked, if for no other reason than how I looked and behaved would reflect upon Papa and Maman. All of us wanted to make a good impression on Monsieur LeGrand.

"My dress isn't too wrinkled, is it?" I asked anxiously, and felt the butterflies settle down a little when it was Celeste who answered.

"You look just fine."

"The young ladies' presence is requested in the

parlor," our housekeeper, Marie Louise, announced from the bedroom door. Marie Louise's back is always as straight as a ruler, and her skirts are impeccably starched. She cast a critical eye over the three of us, then gave a satisfied nod.

"What does Monsieur LeGrand look like, Marie Louise?" I asked. "Did you see him? Tell us!"

Marie Louise gave a sniff to show she disapproved of such questions, though her eyes were not unkind.

"Of course I saw him," she answered, "for who was it who answered the door? But I don't have time to stand around gossiping any more than you have time to stand around and listen. Get along with you, now. Your parents and Monsieur LeGrand are waiting for you in the parlor."

With a rustle of skirts, she left.

My sisters and I looked at one another for a moment, as if catching our collective breath.

"Come on," Celeste said. And, just like that, she was off. April followed hard on her heels.

"Celeste," I begged, my feet screaming in agony as I tried to keep up. "Don't go so fast. Slow down."

But I was talking to the open air, for my sisters were already gone. By the time I made it to the bedroom door, they were at the top of the stairs. And by the time I made it to the top of the stairs, they were at the bottom. Celeste streaked across the entryway, then paused before the parlor door, just long enough to give her curls a brisk shake and clasp her hands in front of her as was proper. Then, without a backward glance, she marched straight into the parlor with April trailing along behind her.

Slowly, I descended the stairs, then came to a miserable stop in the downstairs hall.

Should I go forward, I wondered, *or should I stay right where I am?*

No matter who got taken to task over our entry later—and someone most certainly would be—there could be no denying that I was the one who would look bad at present. I was the one who was late. I'd probably already embarrassed my parents and insulted our honored guest. *Perhaps I should simply slink away, back to my room*, I thought. I could claim I'd suddenly become ill between the top of the stairs and the bottom, that it was in everyone's best interest that I hadn't made an appearance, particularly Monsieur LeGrand's.

And perhaps I could flap my arms and fly to the moon.

That's when I heard the voices drifting out of the parlor.

There was Maman's, high and piping like a flute. Papa's with its quiet ebb and flow that always reminds me of the sea. Celeste and April I could not hear at all, of course. They were children and would not speak unless spoken to first. And then I heard a voice like the great rumble of distant thunder say:

"But where is la petite Belle?"

And, just as real thunder will sometimes inspire my feet to carry me from my own room into my parents', so too the sound of what could be no other than Monsieur LeGrand's voice carried me through the parlor door and into the room beyond. As if to make up for how slowly my feet had moved before, I overshot my usual place in line. Instead of ending up at the end of the row, next to April, I came to a halt between my two sisters. April was to my left and Celeste to my right. We were out of order for the first and only time in our lives.

I faltered, appalled. For I was more than simply out of place, I was also directly in front of Monsieur LeGrand.

Nonboring, Nonpreachy:
Nonfiction

From Simon Pulse | Published by Simon & Schuster